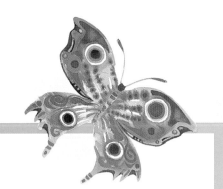

The Best Children's Books in the World

A Treasury of Illustrated Stories

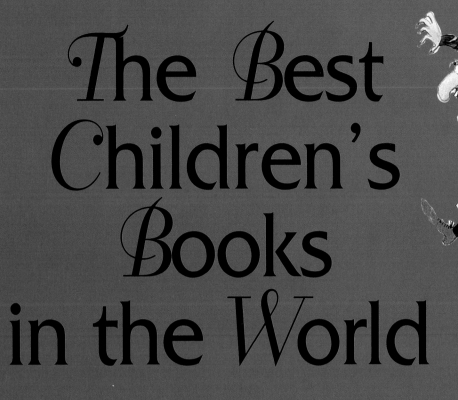

The Best Children's Books in the World

A Treasury of Illustrated Stories

EDITED BY

BYRON PREISS

KATHY HUCK, PROJECT EDITOR

INTRODUCTION BY

JEFFREY GARRETT

A BYRON PREISS BOOK

HARRY N. ABRAMS, INC., PUBLISHERS

This book is dedicated to
Karah and Blaire Preiss,
Madeline Hardy,
and all the other children in our world.

For Byron Preiss Visual Publications, Inc.:
Designer: Gilda Hannah
Editorial Assistants: Elham Cohanim and Robin Ambrosino

For Harry N. Abrams, Inc.:
Project Manager: Harriet Whelchel
Design Consultant: Robert McKee

Library of Congress Cataloging-in-Publication Data

The best children's books in the world : a treasury of illustrated
stories / edited by Byron Preiss ; Kathy Huck, associate editor;
introduction by Jeffrey Garrett.
p.   cm.
"A Byron Preiss book."
Summary: A collection of illustrated stories, originally published
separately, from all over the world.
ISBN 0–8109–1246–5 (cloth)/ISBN 0–8109–2383–1 (pbk.)
1. Children's stories. [1. Short stories.] I. Preiss, Byron.
II. Huck, Kathy. III. Garrett, Jeffrey.
PZ5.B422   1996
[Fic]—dc20 96–13651

Printed and bound in Hong Kong

 Harry N. Abrams, Inc.
100 Fifth Avenue
New York, N.Y. 10011
www.abramsbooks.com

CONTENTS

The Many Republics of Childhood

International children's books is a collective term we in America use to refer to all the children's books in the world that are not "ours." In this sense it is a figment, as meaningless an abstraction as the notion of the "international child." There *is* no such thing as an international children's book. Every child's book that is real and not the product of some multinational marketing department arises, like every real child, at the conjunction of a unique time with a unique place. Children's books, or at least the very best of them, such as those collected in this volume, are created in real places to be read by real children with a real and very specific cultural sensorium. There are books in Wolof or French for Senegalese children, in Slovak for the children of Bratislava or Košice, in Spanish for the children of Mexican immigrants in Texas or California. Pick up any one of these books, and you hold in your hands the magic key to a separate universe. In this lies the enormous power and potential appeal of books from other cultures. You may need help or practice in wielding the key or in finding the casket that it unlocks, but, as the little boy in the Grimms' story "The Golden Key" correctly surmises, "there's surely precious things" within.

We too hastily confer the status of "international children's book" on our own works that have attracted a worldwide following, books by Maurice Sendak, Betsy Byars, Sid Fleischman. This makes it easy to project our own assumptions about quality out into the world, never stopping to let the rest of the world speak to us. A (literally) classic example of cultural exchange conceived of as a one-way street is Lewis Carroll's *Alice's Adventures in Wonderland,* which has been translated into virtually all languages of the world and is often held up as proof that children everywhere share common tastes (namely ours) and respond to children's literature in much the same way as our children do. There are dozens and even hundreds of translations into German, French, Russian, and Japanese. There is also a 1911 translation of *Alice* into Swahili and numerous others into distant languages such as Oriya, Bengali, and Hindi. I know of a 1975 *Alice* edition in the Australian aboriginal language of Pitjantjatjara that would seem to confirm the universality of *Alice*'s appeal. But here this whole line of argument begins to unravel. The "aboriginal" *Alice*, for example, turns out to have been commissioned by the Department of Adult Education at the University of Adelaide, and its strikingly authentic "aboriginal" illustrations were created by Byron Sewell—an artist from Texas. It was not created in anticipation of any demand from aboriginal children or their parents but was instead an instrument of cultural hegemonism. Much the same story characterizes many other translations of *Alice*, rendered lovingly into exotic languages by English missionaries or anglicized colonials—much like the Bible and for many of the same reasons. There is no evidence here for the universality of children's tastes or for that romantic abstraction known as the universal child.

Why not for a change go to these many countries and look at the books that are the favorites of children there? Savor their differentness, reflect on the different messages their creators have sought to convey to the next generation, and enjoy forms and conventions of art that are not our own? They just might speak to us after all. For the true appreciation of other cultures begins with a willingness to enter another mind.

This is precisely what the editors of the present volume have undertaken to do, and in my view, they have succeeded with resourcefulness and flair. The writers and artists assembled here speak evocatively, often *provocatively*, of the many different worlds of childhood. Indeed, in the words they write and the images they draw or paint, they support and reinforce the particular variants of childhood their respective societies have chosen to foster, for it is in childhood that the unique values of a culture are passed on from one generation to the next, and children's literature, both printed and oral and in societies both religious and secular, is a vessel of meaning in this process of transfer.

The centrality of childhood as a period of cultural formation and reformation is emerging with force today as a key to understanding the differences between peoples and generations. This is attested to by the current flood of scholarly publications on the topic, books with titles such as *Children and Childhood in Western Society Since 1500; The Knowledge of Childhood in the German Middle Ages;* and *Chinese Views on Childhood*—to name just a few. Most of these works trace their lineage back to the seminal work of Philippe Ariès, published in English in 1962 under the title *Centuries of Childhood: A Social History of Family Life,* and ultimately back to those original propagandizers of the importance of childhood, Jean-Jacques Rousseau and John Locke.

Scholarly as this new respect for childhood may be, the issue concerns us all. If, as Wordsworth wrote, the child is the father of the man, then the way children are regarded, treated, and raised in the various cultures of our planet, today and in the past, must explain in some measure what these cultures have become and will yet become over time. As Paul Hazard wrote, "We can disregard the literature for childhood only if we consider unimportant the way in which a national soul is formed and sustained."

Here is but one example to show the burning relevance of children's reading for the development of a

culture—and even the maintenance of world peace. In an interview with the journal *Bookbird* in the spring of 1994, the Bosnian children's poet Josip Osti reflected on the long-term implications of his country's horrific civil war for children and the future of the Balkans. In the course of his own work with Bosnian children in refugee camps in Slovenia, Osti observed a greater resilience in those Bosnian children who "cultivated their cultural needs earlier in life." He sees the future of the Balkans hinging in part on what these children will be given to read in the future. Will it be an "ethnically cleansed" literature? Will a "rigidly nationalistic criterion" be forced upon the books read by Serb, Croat, and Muslim children? If this is allowed, then, according to Osti, "the effects will be even more persistent and enduring than the physical destruction as a legacy of the present war." The preconditions for international, transcultural, and transethnic understanding include prominently an appreciation for the validity of the cultures of others. And books are a very compact and highly mobile source for engendering precisely this kind of appreciation.

There is an encouraging historical precedent for this process of engendering understanding. In 1945, a German Jew named Jella Lepman returned to her native country, in full cognizance of what had happened to her own family at the hands of the Nazis. Her mission was to help ensure that a new generation of German children had new books to read and new versions of the truth to choose from. Her vision of the formative power of children's reading was shared by Eleanor Roosevelt, Mildred Batchelder of the American Library Association, and a host of world publishers who responded to her call to build a bridge of children's books to the children of the vanquished Nazi state. It was, among other things, the birth moment of the International Youth Library in Munich and of IBBY, the International Board on Books for Young People, which today still awards its Hans Christian Andersen Medal and other commendations to the great children's writers and illustrators of the world—including several represented on the pages of this book. To this day, Germany is one of very few countries in the world that regularly consider books in translation for their most prestigious annual book award, the Jugendliteraturpreis—the equivalent of our Newbery. Many of these books have won.

It should be remembered that the authors and artists represented in this volume, though "speaking" to us here in English translation, first sought a dialogue with the children of their own culture. Yet by participating in this dialogue—eavesdropping, as it were—we may not only broaden our own horizons and those of our children but, as an unexpected reward, also reach a better comprehension of what is uniquely characteristic in our own culture. Since the United States is a country of immigrants, we will encounter elements of other cultures that have gone into making ours. We will find tales which may seem very much at home in our cultural context, such as Carl Norac's *The Braggart Lion* from Belgium, with illustrations by Frédéric de Bus, or Martin Waddell's *The Hidden House*, illustrated by Angela Barrett. Others, however, speak different truths in aesthetic languages very different from the Western mainstream, for example, *The Legend of the Palm Tree and the Goat* from Iran, extraordinarily illustrated by Sara Iravani in a style possessing all the magical power and vitality of cave paintings, or Meshack Asare's simple but unmistakably African *Cat in Search of a Friend*. Enticingly foreign to our experience is also the dramatic and elegantly stylized Maori legend *Paikea*, by Robyn Kahukiwa of New Zealand, and Sybil Wettasinghe's swirling folkloristic *The Umbrella Thief*, which incidentally first made its mark in Japan before coming to the United States. Contributors from Europe include masters of styles of the classical mainstream, such as the meticulous and eclectic Russians Andrej Dugin and Olga Dugina, whose *Dragon Feathers* evokes Albrecht Dürer, Lucas Cranach, and other masters of the Northern Renaissance—especially Hieronymus Bosch. From Europe, there are also modern artists in search of new visual languages, the brilliant Slovak surrealist Dušan Kállay, for example, who still owes a debt to Bosch (but perhaps even more to Pieter Brueghel). While these artists may strike us as more "adult" and "civilized," others have visibly allied themselves with children as "that greatest of savage tribes," as Douglas Newton has called them. In this category we can place the Israeli artist Ora Ayal in *Five Wacky Witches*, Brazil's Angela Lago in *Street Scene*, and the Russian artist Andrey Martynov with his images for *Bad Advice*. Finally, gifted Catalans Carme Solé Vendrell and Miquel Obiols continue the rich European tradition of allegorical fantasy—the tradition of Saint-Exupéry's *The Little Prince*, of Calvino and Lem—with their own haunting tale of outer (and inner) space discovery, *All the Colors in the Rainbow*.

Collected here is an entire rainbow not only of art but of story as well, from the somber and serious to the subversive and even downright silly. Taken together, as they are in this anthology, these stories are as rich and as variegated as the world of childhood itself. If there is any common denominator to them at all, it is to be found in the love and respect they show for children as the authors of our shared future.

JEFFREY GARRETT

LE LION
FANFARON

Carl Norac - Frédéric du Bus

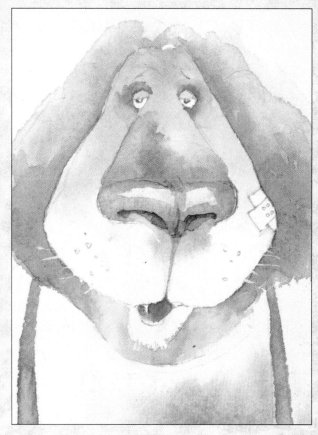

p a g i v o r e s

casterman

The Braggart Lion (Le Lion Fanfaron)

WRITTEN BY CARL NORAC

TRANSLATED BY CARY RYAN

ILLUSTRATED BY FRÉDÉRIC DE BUS

Strawberry, the planet's most modest lion, would have liked to remain silent on the subject of his extraordinary self. But he thought it would be cruel to ignore the thousands of admirers who had written to inquire about the story of his life. In *The Braggart Lion,* he recounts for his fans his mercurial rise to greatness. But, in this sophisticated, irreverant, and ironic work, it is Frédéric de Bus's humorous illustrations that tell the *real* story—and the juxtaposition between the text and the artwork is hilariously entertaining. From his "prestigious" genealogical tree to his "fearless" travels around the world to his discovery of "true love," Strawberry's imagination makes for a great—if somewhat exaggerated—memoir.

Carl Norac was born in 1960 in Mons, Belgium. A professor of French, screenplay writer, cartoonist, and journalist, Norac is also widely known for his poetry; two collections of his works have received international acclaim. In 1986, Mr. Norac decided to try children's-book writing and has since written at least twelve titles. His stories are often humorous, nonsensical but tender in tone. He presently lives on a farm in Montignies-les-Lens, a small village in the Belgian Hainaut, surrounded by willows and malicious cats.

Born in 1963 in Brussels, Belgium, Frédéric de Bus studied design at the Saint-Luc Institute in Brussels and has been working as an illustrator since 1988. In addition to his work for children's magazines, he is a political cartoonist for a number of Belgian newspapers. He continues to live and work in Brussels.

Dear Readers,

I, Strawberry, the most modest lion on the planet, would just as soon never breathe a word about My Extraordinary Self. But how cruel it would be to disappoint the millions of admirers who have written Me in hopes of having the great honor of hearing the Story of My Life.

If you are reading this letter, you must have bought My book. At least, I hope you have, for memories, like toothbrushes, should never be borrowed. (I came up with that line Myself!) Either way, let me assure you that every penny of the proceeds from the book will go directly to the Friends of Strawberry charity, of which I am the honorary president and treasurer. It is my dearest wish that My heroic career might serve as an example not only to today's youth but to all future generations.

I roar you a kiss.

Strawberry

My family can trace its lineage back to Adam. In fact, even before there were humans or, for that matter, diplodocuses, My ancestors invented (in six days, six hours, six minutes, and six seconds): fire, the wheel, the apple, the T-shirt, the arch, and even the boomerang.

Chers lecteurs,

Moi, Strawberry, le lion
le plus modeste de la planète,
J'aurais voulu rester discret
sur Mes immenses mérites.
Mais il Me serait cruel de décevoir
les milliers d'admirateurs qui M'ont écrit
pour avoir le grand honneur de connaître
l'Histoire de Ma Vie.
Vous lisez cette lettre, vous avez donc acheté
Mon Livre. Du moins, Je l'espère,
car les Mémoires sont comme les brosses à dents,
elles ne se prêtent pas. (C'est de Moi !)
De toute manière, soyez rassurés, les bénéfices
de l'ouvrage seront intégralement versés à l'œuvre
de charité "Les Amis de Strawberry" dont
Je suis le Président d'Honneur et le Trésorier.
Que Mon Destin de Héros serve d'exemple
à la jeunesse d'aujourd'hui et aux générations
des siècles à venir : tel est Mon Vœu le plus cher.

Je vous rugis un baiser.

Strawberry

Ma famille remonte à Adam.
Bien avant les hommes ou les diplodocus,
Mon ancêtre a inventé, en six jours, six heures,
six minutes et six secondes, le feu, la roue,
la pomme, le tee-shirt, l'arc et même la flèche-
boomerang.

Mon arbre généalogique est donc si haut
qu'il chatouille les branches des étoiles.
(C'est de Moi !)
Depuis toujours, dans la famille, nous avons
la coquetterie d'être roi de père en fils.
L'un des Nôtres, Richard Cœur de Lion, participa
à la Troisième Croisade. Il triompha même
par 3 buts à 0 contre l'équipe nationale
de Mésopotamie dont le coach était
Salah al-Din Yusuf dit Saladin Ier.

My genealogical tree is so tall it tickles the stars. (I came up with that line Myself!) From time immemorial, the title of king has passed down from father to son in my family. One of us, Richard the Lion-Hearted, led the Third Crusade and triumphed, by three goals to nothing, over the National Mesopotamian Team, coached by Saladin.

De tous les temps, Nos Aïeux ont brillé
par leur bravoure et leur élégance.
Mon père, Chevalier de la Bretelle, Nous éleva
dans le respect des grandes traditions propres
aux fauves à la noble crinière.
Très tôt, il Nous apprit à porter l'armure
et le casque.

From the very beginning, My ancestors distinguished themselves by their bravery and their flair. My father, Chevalier of Bretelle, brought us up with respect for the great traditions befitting beasts of the noble mane. We were still cubs when he taught us to wear armor and battle helmets.

At the tenderest age, I was admitted to the best schools. Was I exceptional? The word is does not begin to do Me justice. My mind bounded from class to class like a gazelle on the Russian steppes. (I came up with that line Myself!) My fellow students wept with envy at the spectacle of my brilliance. I was awarded so many honors I lost count.

Je fus bientôt admis, brillamment, dans les plus Grandes Ecoles. Surdoué, Moi ? Le mot est faible... Mon esprit bondissait de classe en classe comme une gazelle dans la savane rousse. (C'est de Moi !) Les copains de l'Ecole pleuraient d'envie devant les mille feux de Mon intelligence.
Que de couronnes de lauriers ai-Je collectionnées !

Après les lauriers, Je Me mis à collectionner les diplômes comme d'autres les timbres-poste, les ailes d'alligator ou les sacs pure peau de zèbre à pois.
Ainsi, Je devins Docteur, Architecte, Philosophe, Fort des Halles et Grand-Maître-Coiffeur des Crinières Royales.
Pour Me proposer un contrat, les employeurs des grandes villes faisaient la queue.

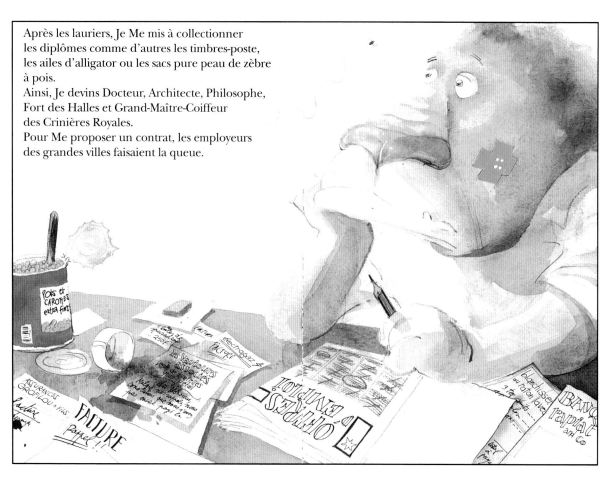

After the honors, I set about collecting diplomas the way others collect postage stamps, alligator wings, or purses made from the hides of polka-dotted zebras.

I became a doctor, an architect, a philosopher, a strongman, and Master Groomer of the Royal Manes. Big-city bosses stood in line to offer Me contracts.

*Newspaper reads: HELP WANTED

Trop de travail tue les âmes bien nées.
(C'est de Moi!)
J'avais besoin de silence et de paix.
Alors, écoutant battre comme un tambour
Mon cœur de patriote, Je me suis engagé
sous la bannière de Sa Majesté.
Dès Mon arrivée, chacun reconnut en Moi
l'âme d'un vrai chef.

Too much work destroys the highborn soul. (I came up with that line Myself!)

I needed peace and quiet.

So, heeding the drumbeat of My patriotic heart, I enlisted under Her Majesty's colors. Right from the start, everyone acknowledged that I had the soul of a true leader.

Je gravis les grades comme d'autres un escalier.
As des missions secrètes, confident des stratèges,
Je fus nommé Amiral du plus grand porte-avions
de la Flotte Royale.
Un jour, un jeune mousse, sentant sa fin prochaine,
Me dit en balbutiant:
— Amiral, un soir, vous coulerez sous le poids
des médailles.
Je compris que Mon destin était ailleurs.
La mort dans l'âme, Je quittai les Armes.
Mais déjà, Je nourrissais un petit projet qui,
depuis six marées, Me chatouillait la crinière:
CONQUERIR LE MONDE

I climbed through the ranks as others climb stairways. Ace of spies and a confidant of the top brass, I was named admiral of the largest aircraft carrier in the Royal Fleet.

One day, a young midshipman, sensing that the end was near, stammered: "Admiral, one night, you will sink under the weight of your own medals." I understood that my destiny lay elsewhere. Sick at heart, I left the military. But even then, I was entertaining a little project that had been tickling My fancy for many moons: CONQUERING THE WORLD.

I traveled across fields and deserts, seas and corridors. In Arabia, I was made an emir, in the Sahara, a maharaja. When I was elected Prince of the Sands, eager porters, sweating and stumbling, carried Me from the Palace of Delights to the Green Oasis.

Je traversai dès lors les terres et les déserts, les mers, les corridors.
En Arabie, Je fus Emir, Maharadjah au Sahara.
Elu Prince des Sables, Je fus véhiculé par des porteurs zélés, suants et trébuchants, du Palais des Délices aux Vertes Oasis.

In country after country, I met the most important people. Everywhere, I was welcomed as an artist and appointed to the highest posts. Russia gave Me *carte blanche* ("a white card," meaning I could do it my way!) to repaint the Red Square.

America gave Me a "red card" to repaint the White House.

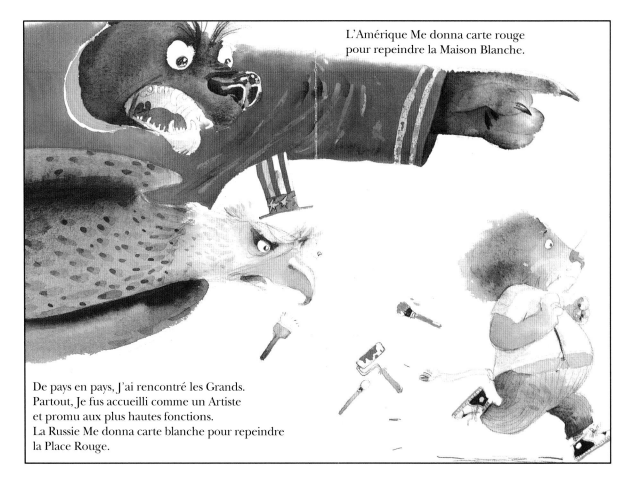

L'Amérique Me donna carte rouge pour repeindre la Maison Blanche.

De pays en pays, J'ai rencontré les Grands.
Partout, Je fus accueilli comme un Artiste et promu aux plus hautes fonctions.
La Russie Me donna carte blanche pour repeindre la Place Rouge.

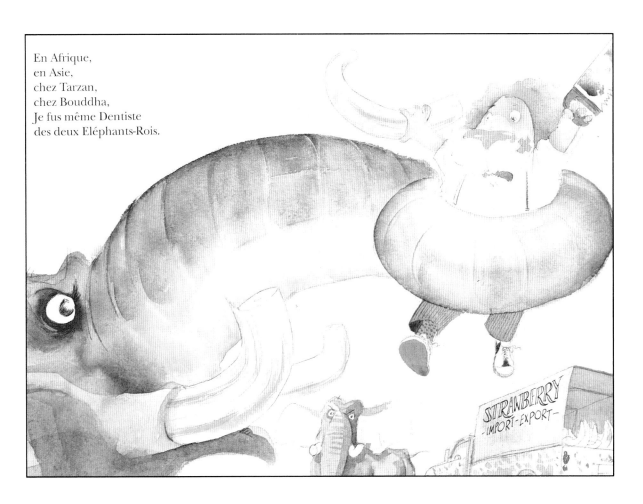

En Afrique,
en Asie,
chez Tarzan,
chez Bouddha,
Je fus même Dentiste
des deux Eléphants-Rois.

In Africa and Asia, I hobnobbed with Tarzan and the Buddha. I even became dentist to two elephant kings.

Moi, Strawberry le Conquérant,
Je n'avais pas encore connu la Vraie Vie...
Ce matin-là, un événement allait changer
Mon destin.
Dès l'aube écarlate, Je Me levai de la patte gauche,
celle du cœur. Mon pouls se mit à battre tel Big-Ben.
Je sus que ce jour-là serait Mon jour de chance.
Il y a des signes qui ne trompent pas.

I, Strawberry, had conquered the world, but I had not yet truly lived.

One morning, something happened that would change My life.

At the break of a scarlet dawn, I got out of bed on My left paw, the one closest to My heart. My pulse beat like the great London clock Big Ben.

Some signs are unmistakable. I knew that this would be My lucky day.

Love descended upon Me like a shower of angels into a pool of ink. (I came up with that line Myself!)

I had gone to do some shopping, and so had milady. I was in a bit of a rush, and so was milady. I flirted with her a little, and she flirted back. I brushed against her, and she brushed back.

And then we were seized by a trembling passion. I roared. She blushed.

She had had only to look into My eyes to fall in love with Me.

Ainsi, l'Amour M'est tombé sur la crinière
comme une pluie d'anges dans une mare d'encre.
(C'est de moi!)
J'étais allé faire quelques emplettes, Milady aussi.
J'étais un peu pressé, Milady aussi.
Je l'ai un peu pressée, Milady aussi.
Je l'ai un peu heurtée, Milady aussi.

Alors nous fûmes pris d'un Saint Tremblement.
Je rugis. Elle rougit.
Ne contemplant que Mes yeux, elle M'aima.

Her name was Lady Racket. Her father was the Indian consul. Her mother was a fighter pilot. I was her Romeo. She became My Juliet. She was My blueberry, I, her wild strawberry.

Elle s'appelait Lady Racket.
Son père était Consul des Indes.
Sa mère était Pilote de Chasse.
J'étais son Roméo.
Elle devint Ma Juliette.
Elle était Ma myrtille;
Moi, sa fraise des bois.

Chers lecteurs, Je vous livre en exclusivité
mondiale le cliché que Lord Sundown,
Photographe Royal, a tiré de Notre Mariage.
De nombreux carnivores, et quelques
Pachydermes Nous ont accompagnés,
nobles et fiers, jusqu'à l'Abbaye de Westminster.

Dear readers, I am now going to let you in on the exclusive world premiere of the photographs the royal photographer, Lord Sundown, took at our wedding.

Numerous carnivores and even some pachyderms, all noble and proud, accompanied us to Westminster Abbey.

Notre voyage de noces se passa dans les plus
grands palaces. Couchés sur des sofas de soie,
Nous y dégustions les mets les plus délicats.
Quand on aime, on ne compte pas.
(Ce n'est pas de moi!)

Mais déjà, à l'époque,
Lady Strawberry était très économe.

We spent our honeymoon in the grandest palaces. Lounging on silk sofas, we savored delicacy after delicacy after delicacy. When one is in love, one loses count. (I did *not* come up with that line Myself!)

But already, Lady Strawberry exhibited a frugal streak.

*Label reads: SECOND-RATE ORANGES

Youth of today, I hope you will allow Me to pass on to you the secret of the perfect marriage. First, the husband must stay in his place (preferably by the fireside). And second, the wife must remember that a lion is nothing but a big pussycat.

Symbols of the ideal union, My wife and I looked forward to unending happiness.

However . . .

Jeunesse d'aujourd'hui, qu'il Me soit permis de vous enseigner les deux règles d'une union exemplaire:
Un: Le mâle doit garder sa place (la meilleure, près du feu).
Deux: L'épouse doit savoir qu'un lion n'a pas de corne.
Symboles du mariage idéal, Nous Nous préparions à un bonheur sans fin.
Cependant...

...Un après-midi, brusquement, tout se brisa.
Lors d'un week-end romantique sur la côte,
Ma belle, Mon adorée, disparut. Mystérieusement!
Nul ne l'a plus revue.

Abruptly, one afternoon, the bubble burst. After a romantic weekend at the seashore, My darling disappeared. Mysteriously. No one has seen her since.

*Signs read: DANGER! UNSTABLE CLIFF and DO NOT LEAN OVER

Et depuis ce jour-là,
Je suis INCONSOLABLE...

And since that day, I have
been INCONSOLABLE.

Street Scene
(Cena de Rua)

ILLUSTRATED BY ANGELA LAGO

There is no text in *Street Scene*, but there is certainly a story. Created as a visual report on the homeless, the book depicts a day in the life of a boy who is trying to sell fruit in the street. Angela Lago has illustrated the tale with strong acrylic colors and bold brushstrokes that show her sympathy for street children. "I didn't use any details except those strictly necessary for the report. I didn't want to distract the reader in this book."

Lago also used many design elements to convey her message. Take note of the gutter, which she has used to accentuate the emotion and movement of the drawings. For instance, on page 24 (top spread), she put the elbow and knee of the boy in motion exactly where the two pages come together. And on page 28 (bottom spread), she used the gutter to add perspective in the deepest corners of buildings.

With its innovative design and artistic excellence, it is not suprising that this book has won many awards, including the award for Best Picture Book in 1994 from the Brazilian Section of IBBY and the award for Best Picture Book in 1994 from the APCA (the Association of Critics and Journalists).

Angela Lago lives and works in Belo Horizonte, Brazil, where she was born in 1945. Having earned a degree in social work, she worked with children for many years in Brazil. In 1972, she went to Edinburgh, Scotland, to study graphic design. As an illustrator, Lago has experimented with her artwork throughout her career: she has pioneered the use of computer-generated images in books as well as paper-folding and cutout techniques. In 1994, she was nominated for the Hans Christian Andersen Award.

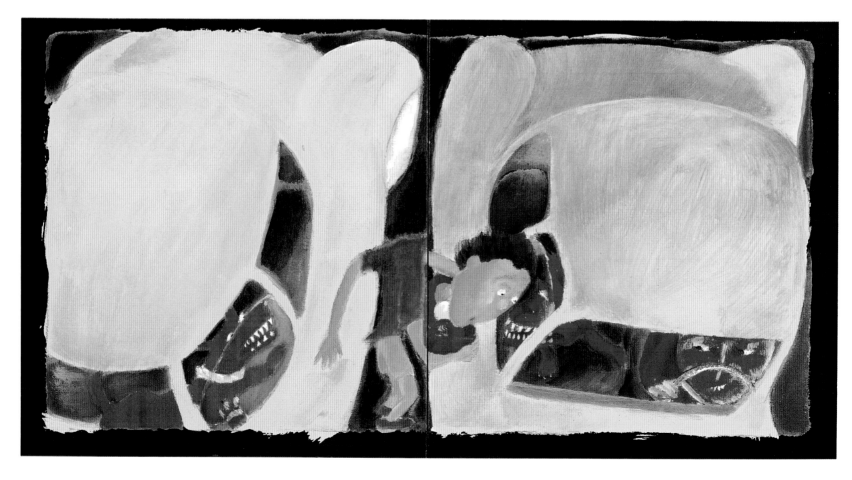

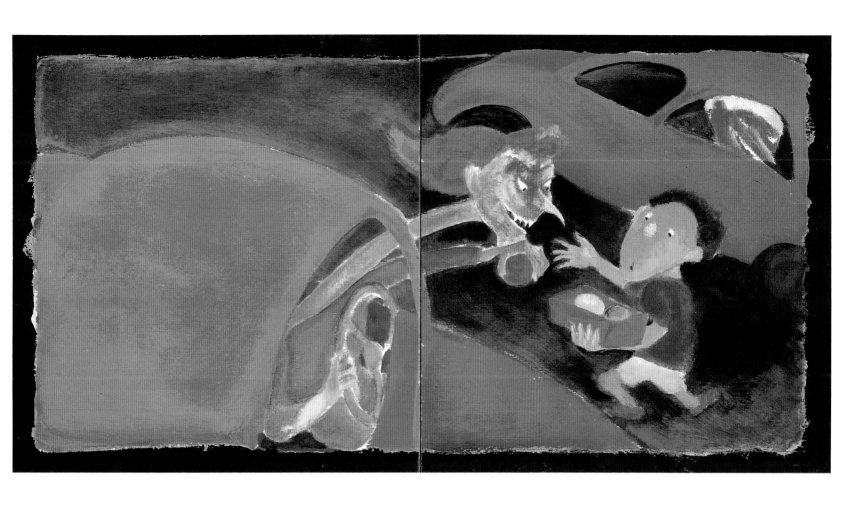

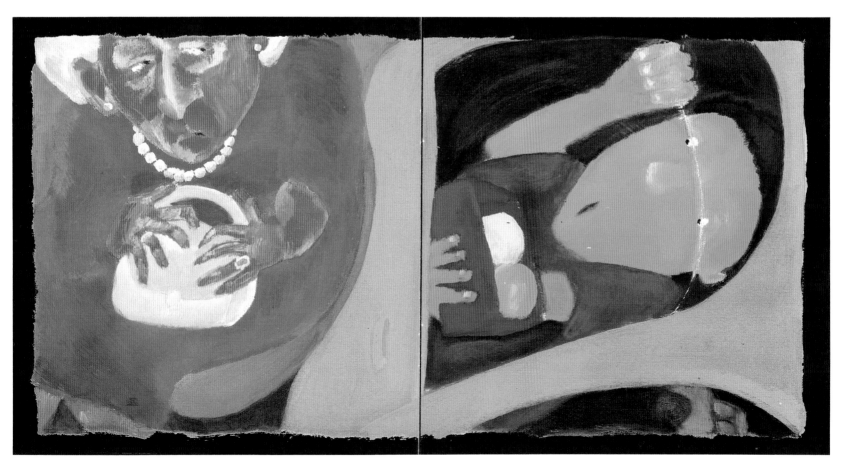

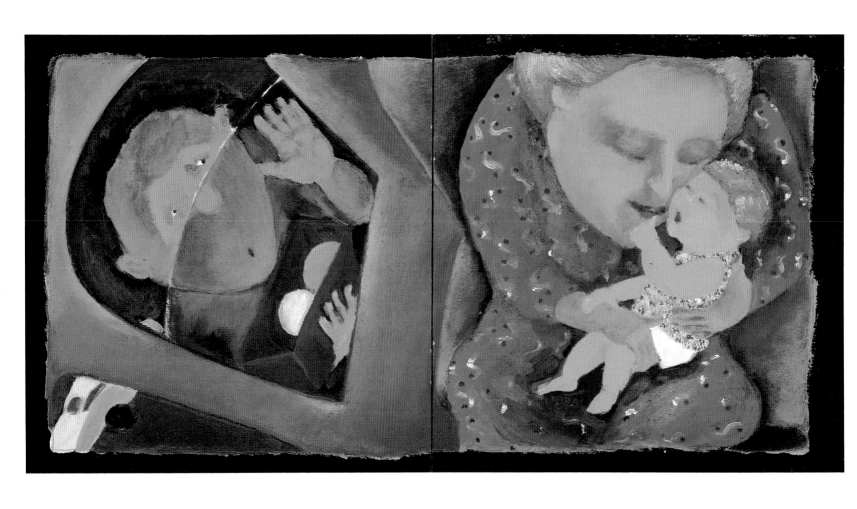

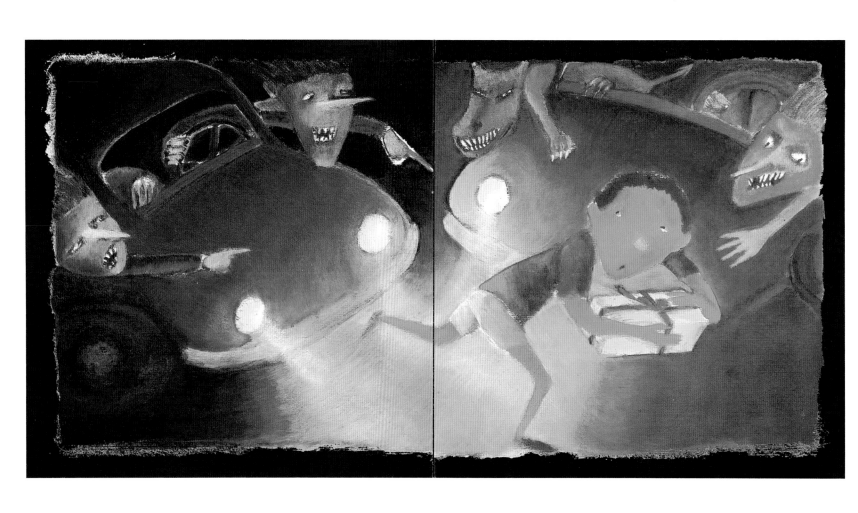

幼学启蒙丛书

中国寓言故事

纪昌学射箭

● 明天出版社

Jichang Learns to Shoot Arrows

FROM *ANCIENT CHINESE FABLES*

WRITTEN BY LIE YUKOU

REWRITTEN BY ZHAO ZHENWAN

TRANSLATED BY SASHA XINYAN MAI

ILLUSTRATED BY LI XUEMING

Li Xueming, who illustrated the short story "Jichang Learns to Shoot Arrows," pays homage to his ancestral masters by using Chinese ink and watercolors on yellow silk—a traditional Chinese technique. His reverence for the cultural past led him to imitate the pure and spare elegant scrolls typical of the Song and Tang dynasties to illustrate the story, which is also ancient in origin. This combination results in a beautiful fusion between ancient literature and art.

The story originated from "Lie Zi," written by Lie Yukou, a Daoist scholar in China sometime in the first millenium B.C., and was rewritten in modern Chinese by Zhao Zhenwan. Although the story had been translated in English, it seemed only appropriate to retain the original Chinese as well, for the text stands on its own as a piece of artistic value.

"Jichang Learns to Shoot Arrows" is a traditional story that gives readers a message while entertaining them. People can finally reach their goals through hard work, perseverance, and loyalty. This retelling of the ancient story proves that such values stand the test of time and cultural differences.

Ancient Chinese Fables is part of The Enlightening Chinese Children Series, a series of books that celebrate ancient Chinese literature. Many of the stories in *Ancient Chinese Fables,* and the poems in a companion book, are by the best and most influential of ancient China's writers. The entire series won the Chinese Excellent Children's Reading Prize in 1990, which is jointly awarded by China's National Cultural Ministry, National Education Committee, and other prestigious organizations. The series also won the First National Book Prize in 1992, which is considered to be the most important book award in China. The illustrations won the Encouraging Prize at the Fourth Children's Book Illustration Exhibition of the Noma Concours held in Tokyo by the Asian Cultural Center of UNESCO.

Zhenwan is vice-president of the Chinese Institute for Children's Reading Research and was chief of China's delegation to the twenty-fifth conference of IBBY. Artist Li Xueming's works have been shown at the National Fine Arts Works Exhibition and other international illustration exhibitions in Tokyo and Bologna.

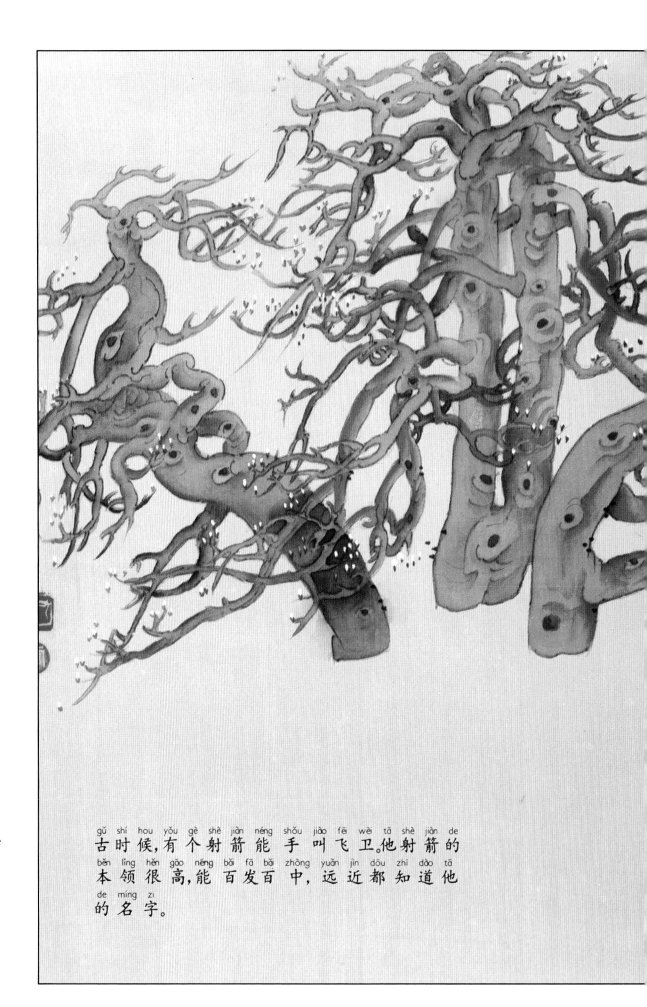

Once upon a time, there lived a brilliant archer named Fei Wei. His archery skills were so superb that his name was known far and wide.

gǔ shí hou yǒu gè shè jiàn néng shǒu jiào fēi wèi tā shè jiàn de
古 时 候, 有 个 射 箭 能 手 叫 飞 卫。他 射 箭 的
běn lǐng hěn gāo néng bǎi fā bǎi zhòng yuǎn jìn dōu zhī dào tā
本 领 很 高, 能 百 发 百 中, 远 近 都 知 道 他
de míng zi
的 名 字。

A young man named Jichang wanted to become a great archer. He went to ask Fei Wei to become his master and teach him archery.

yǒu gè jiào jì chāng de qīng nián wén míng lái bài fēi wèi wéi shī xiàng fēi wèi xué shè jiàn
有个叫纪昌的青年,闻名来拜飞卫为师,向飞卫学射箭。

Fei Wei said to him: "To learn archery, one has to overcome many difficulties. First, excellent eyesight is required. When your eyes are fixed on a target, they must never blink. Go home and master this technique before you come back."

fēi wèi duì tā shuō xué shè jiàn bù néng pà kùn nán shǒu xiān yào liàn hǎo yǎn lì dīng
飞卫对他说:"学射箭不能怕困难,首先要练好眼力,盯
zhe yī gè mù biāo hòu yǎn pí yī zhǎ yě bù zhǎ nǐ huí qù liàn huì le zhè yī diǎn zài lái
着一个目标后,眼皮一眨也不眨。你回去练会了这一点再来。"

Upon returning home, Jichang lay under his wife's loom. He never took his eyes off the shuttle as it went back and forth.

jǐ chāng huí dào ·jiā lǐ
纪昌 回到 家里，
wèi le liàn yǎn lì jiù zuān dào
为了练眼力，就钻到
qī zi de zhī bù jī dǐ xià liǎng
妻子的织布机底下，两
yǎn jǐn dīng zhe chuān lái chuān
眼紧盯着穿来穿
qù de suō zi
去的梭子。

zhè yàng liàn le liǎng nián jí shǐ yǒu rén yòng zhēn qù zhuī tā de yǎn pí tā yě yì zhǎ

这样 练了两 年，即使有人用 针去锥他的眼皮，他也一眨

bù zhǎ

不眨。

In two years, his eyes would not have blinked even if someone had poked his eyelids.

纪昌高高兴兴地去找飞卫,对他说自己已经练得差不多了,该向
他传授射箭的技术了。

Elated, Jichang went back to Fei Wei and told him that he had mastered the technique and it was time for Master Fei to teach him the skills of archery.

fēi wèi què shuō zhè hái bù gòu nǐ huí qù
飞卫 却 说:"这还不够,你回去,
hái děi néng bǎ xiǎo dōng xi kàn dà le zài lái zhǎo wǒ
还得能把小东西看大了,再来找我。"

Fei Wei replied, "Oh, this is not enough. Now you must go home and learn to see small things as though they were big. Then come back and look for me."

Jichang returned home and hung an ant by a hair at the window. All he did every day was stare at the ant.

jì chāng yòu huí dào jiā lǐ yòng yì gēn tóu fà shuān zhe yì zhī mǎ yǐ diào zài chuāng
纪昌 又 回 到 家 里，用 一 根 头 发 栓 着 一 只 蚂 蚁，吊 在 窗
kǒu měi tiān jǐn jǐn dīng zhe nà zhī mǎ yǐ kàn
口，每 天 紧 紧 盯 着 那 只 蚂 蚁 看。

Three years later, the ant became as big as a wheel in Jichang's eyes.

sān nián yǐ hòu zài jì chāng yǎn li mǎ yǐ jìng dà de xiàng ge chē lún
三 年 以 后，在 纪 昌 眼 里，蚂 蚁 竟 大 得 像 个 车 轮。

This time, when Jichang went back to Fei Wei, the master nodded his head and said, "Now I can teach you the art of archery."

jì chāng yòu qù zhǎo fēi wèi fēi wèi diǎn diǎn tóu duì tā shuō xiàn zài kě yǐ jiāo nǐ
纪 昌 又 去 找 飞 卫。飞 卫 点 点 头，对 他 说："现 在 可 以 教 你
xué shè jiàn le
学 射 箭 了。"

Master Fei taught Jichang the technique of pulling back and releasing the arrows.

fēi wèi jiāo jǐ chāng zěn yàng lā gōng zěn yàng fàng jiàn
飞卫教纪昌怎样拉弓,怎样放箭。

Jichang then practiced seriously for many more years. Finally he became the excellent archer he had always hoped to be.

纪昌又刻苦练了好几年，终于成了一个百发百中的神箭手。

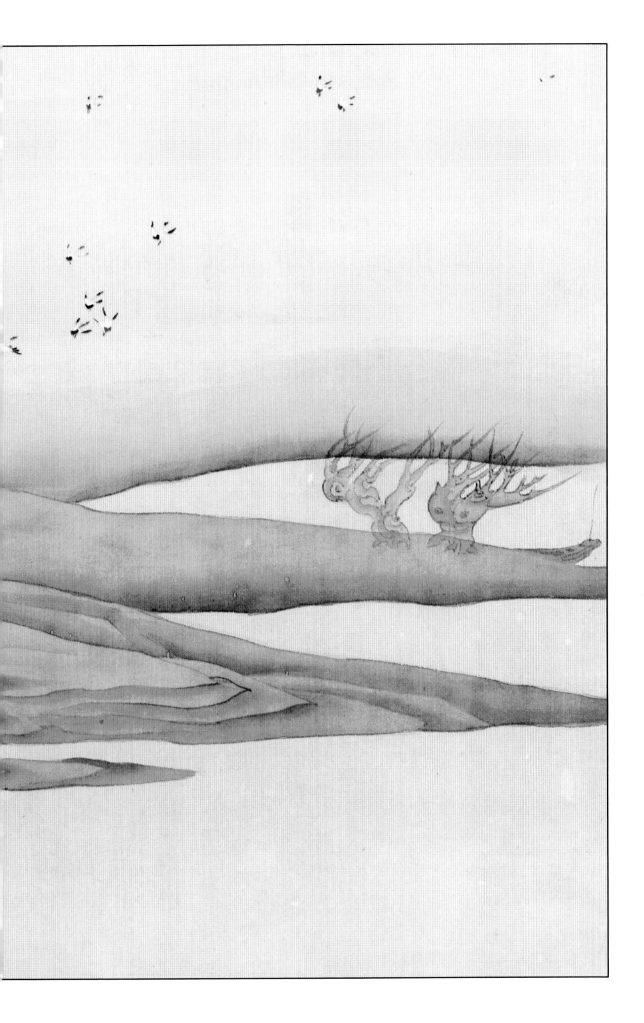

The Hidden House

Martin Waddell & Angela Barrett

The Hidden House

WRITTEN BY MARTIN WADDELL

ILLUSTRATED BY ANGELA BARRETT

While author Martin Waddell was taking his dog for a walk through the back woods of his Northern Ireland home, he came upon something unexpected: a quaint—although delapidated—cottage peeking through the overgrown hedges. That cottage became the inspiration for the delightful tale of *The Hidden House.* He took his story to Walker Books, who asked artist Angela Barrett to illustrate the tale.

Ms. Barrett used her aunt and uncle's three-hundred-year-old cottage in Warwickshire, England, as a model for her illustrations. She further personalized the story by incorporating a few characters from her own life: her black and white cat, and cats belonging to various friends. To evoke the eighteenth-century charm of the house, she borrowed styles from the masters: the scene on page 61, in which the family is seen entering the grounds, was inspired by Graham Sutherland's *Entrance to a Lane,* and the yellow room with the vase of flowers was inspired by Charles Willson Peale's 1795 painting *The Staircase Group.*

Martin Waddell has written more than ninety books, many of which are award-winning picture books. Among them is the internationally acclaimed *Can't You Sleep, Little Bear?* Although he lived briefly in London, Mr. Waddell has now returned to his native home in Newcastle, County Down, Ireland.

Born in Hornchurch, Essex, England, Angela Barrett studied at the Maidstone College of Art and at the Royal College of Art. She started her professional career in periodical illustration, working for such magazines as the *The Sunday Times Magazine, The Observer Magazine,* and *House and Garden.* Her first children's book was *The King, the Cat, and the Fiddle,* published in 1983. Since then she has illustrated numerous children's picture books.

In a little house, down a little lane, lived an old man.

His name was Bruno.

He was very lonely in the little house, so he made wooden dolls to keep him company.

He made three of them. The knitting one is Maisie, the one with the spade is Ralph, and the one with the pack on his back is Winnaker.

They sat on Bruno's window ledge and watched him working in his garden, growing potatoes and cabbages and parsnips and beans.

Bruno talked to them sometimes, but not very much. They were wooden dolls and they couldn't talk back, and Bruno wasn't stupid. The dolls didn't talk, but I *think* they were happy.

One day Bruno went away and didn't come back.

Everything changed, slowly.

Wild things covered the lane and climbed all over Bruno's fence. Brambles choked the garden, and ivy crept in through the window of the little house and spread about inside. A pale tree grew in the kitchen.

Maisie and Ralph and Winnaker watched it happen from their window ledge and they got dusty. They watched and watched, until the spiders spun up their window so that there was nothing left to see but webs. They didn't say anything, because they were wooden dolls, but I *think* they were lonely.

A mouse came by and nibbled Ralph's spade.

A beetle lived in Maisie's basket for a day and then it went away. An ant explored Winnaker but didn't find anything.

Slowly, very slowly (it took years and years and years) Bruno's little house disappeared in the middle of green things.

It was still there, but nobody could see it. The house was hidden, and Maisie and Ralph and Winnaker were hidden inside it. I think they were watching. There was a lot to see in the hidden house.

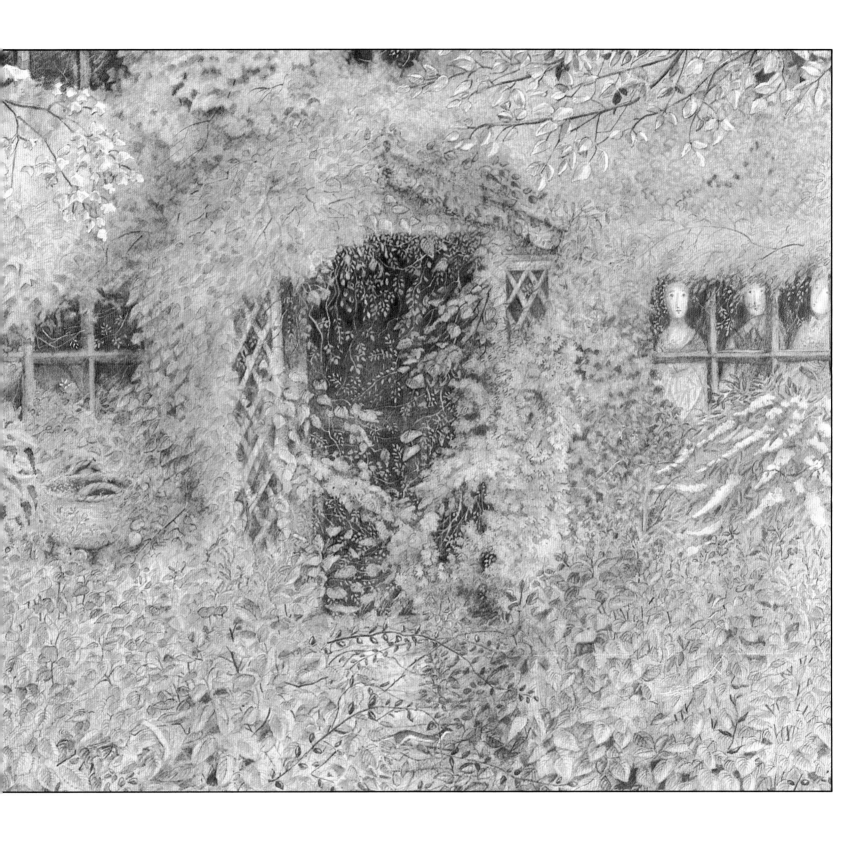

The house filled up with ants and beetles, mice and toads and creepy-crawlies, until it was fuller than it had ever been. Bees buzzed up the chimney, where the smoke used to be.

The little house grew warm and smelly with decay, but it was full of things happening.

Maisie and Ralph and Winnaker got damp and mildewed and turned a bit green, but I don't think they minded too much.

Then a man came down the lane and found the little house by poking his way in through the branches. He didn't spot Maisie and Ralph and Winnaker, because they were hidden in the ivy.

He liked the little house.

Next day he came again with his wife and daughter, and they explored the house and the garden, and liked it very much.

They said they'd come back, but a long time went by and they didn't come.

The hidden house had been forgotten again, and I *think* the wooden dolls were sad.

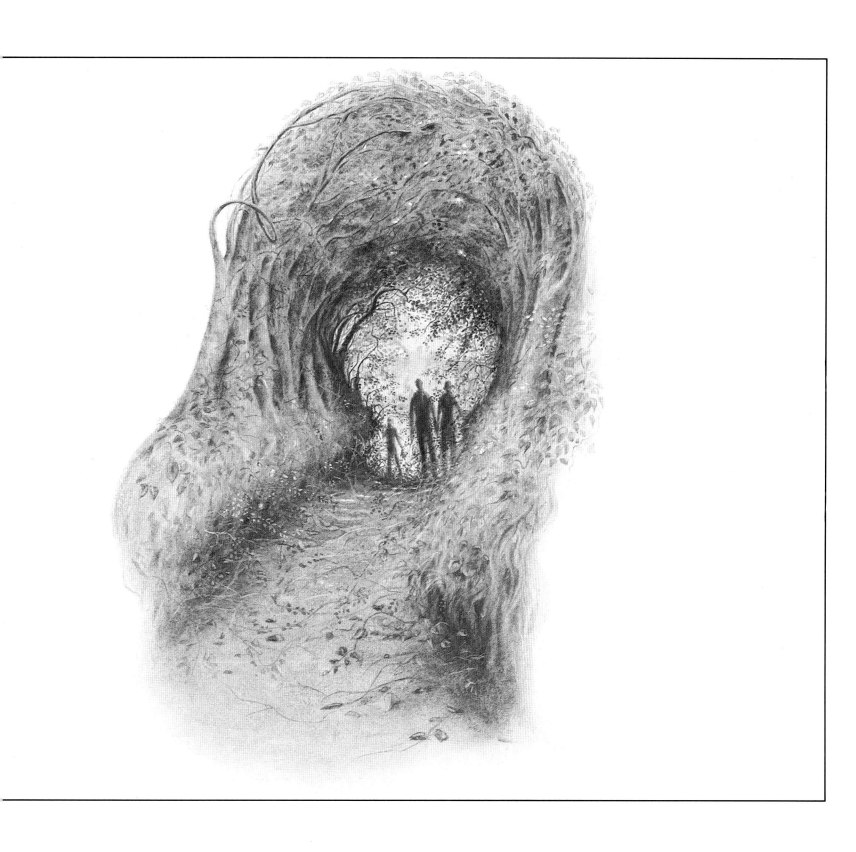

A whole winter
passed and
the house was
covered in snow.
Lots of things came
in from the wood
and hid there,
away from the cold.

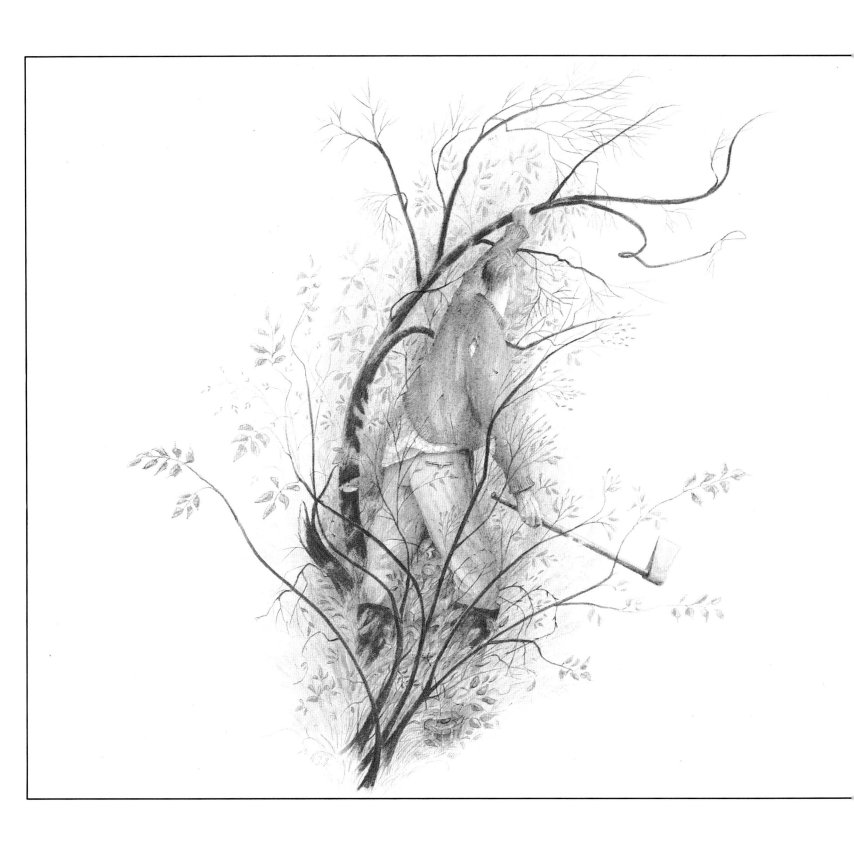

Then, in the spring, the man came back with his wife and his little girl, and he brought a big axe. He cleared away the wildness round the little house. The man

and his wife and the little girl cleaned and cleared and hammered and nailed and painted and washed and brushed and *did* until everything was lovely.

The little girl found Maisie and Ralph and Winnaker. She got her paintbrush and painted them. Then she set them on the window ledge, looking out at the garden. The garden was filled with flowers.

"There you are!" said the little girl. "A whole new world to look at."

"A whole new family for them to look after," said the woman.

"Our family," said the man, and he hugged his wife and daughter.

Maisie and Ralph and Winnaker didn't say a thing. They couldn't. They were wooden dolls. But now they had a whole family to live with, and I *think* they were happy again.

DRAGON FEATHERS

Andrej Dugin and Olga Dugina

Dragon Feathers
(Die Drachenfedern)

RETOLD BY ARNICA ESTERL

ILLUSTRATED BY ANDREJ DUGIN AND OLGA DUGINA

Let us go back in time, to an era when wizards were wise, damsels were in distress, and dragons were ferocious. Full of chivalry and adventure, *Dragon Feathers* retells the classic folktale of a poor woodcutter's son who must pluck three feathers from the wings of a terrible dragon in order to win the hand of the innkeeper's daughter.

Like their contemporary Gennady Spirin, the well-known Russian artist team Andrej Dugin and Olga Dugina pay tribute to the realistic masterpieces of the Renaissance with their lush landscapes and wonderful detail. The oil paintings in this work—in hues of yellow, green, and brown—took two years to finish. But look closely at the illustrations: as realistic and intricate as they are, they contain strange inscriptions and cryptic figures reminiscent of the Dutch painter Hieronymus Bosch's works—mysterious letters, eerie hooded creatures, and the strange morphing of animals. Even the dragon's figure—with the hooves of a goat, human hands, and the feathers of a bird—is an ambiguity. These unusual features give the book an unsettling surrealism, recalling a more enchanting and fantastical time, when things did not necessarily occur with reason. These intricately rendered illustrations will be remembered long after the story from Austria's Ziller Valley has been read.

Andrej Dugin has been painting and illustrating books for more than twenty years, and Olga Dugina has several published works to her credit as well. The two met while Dugin was teaching at the Moscow Art College. They are now married and collaborate on illustrated projects, the first of which was the 1991 retelling of Arnica Esterl's tale *The Fine Round Cake*, which won them critical acclaim. They continue to live in Moscow.

Once upon a time there was a rich innkeeper who had a beautiful daughter. In a hut next to the inn lived a poor woodcutter and his son, Henry. Henry was a sprightly young man, the most handsome lad in the village, and he was honest and hardworking. The boy was always good-humored and busy at some task or other, but whenever he saw Lucy, the innkeeper's daughter, he stopped whatever he was doing and could only stand and stare.

Now, Lucy was also heartsick for the woodcutter's son. Unfortunately, Henry was poor, and Lucy feared that if she asked her father for his blessing, he would refuse. But you never know until you try, and so the bold girl took her beloved before her father and asked if they could marry.

"You foolish girl," roared the innkeeper. And with a cruel laugh he turned to Henry and said, "The only way you can win my Lucy's hand is to go to the dragon of the forest, pull out three of his golden feathers, and bring them back to me."

Henry knew that the dragon was a great sorcerer who destroyed any human in his sight, but heartened by Lucy's bravery, he said he would face the beast. He set off at once for the dragon's castle, which he knew was hidden in a gloomy wood only a day's walk away.

Along the road Henry passed a cottage where a farmer sat crying and moaning, his head buried in his hands. "Why are you so sad?" Henry asked.

"My daughter has been ill for many years, and only one so wise as the dragon could help her, but—"

Henry interrupted, saying, "I'm on my way to the dragon's castle. Perhaps I can ask him what to do. I'll tell you what he says when I return."

The woodcutter's son continued on his way until he came to a wide green meadow, where he saw many people gathered around an apple tree. "Is this tree so beautiful that you all must stand and stare at it?" Henry asked.

A gentleman in the crowd answered: "The tree would certainly please us if it still dropped golden apples as it used to, but now it bears only thorns. If someone were brave enough to go and ask the dragon what has gone wrong, we would pay him handsomely."

"I will speak to the dragon," said Henry, and he set out again.

From the top of the next hill, Henry could see the
dragon's palace shining in the distance, and he quickened
his steps. He soon came to a broad river, where an old
fisherman offered to take him across.

As Henry climbed into the small boat, the man
began to weep.

"What makes you unhappy, fisherman?"
asked Henry.

"I've been forced to pole my boat back and forth
across this wide river all my life, and I am growing weary.
Only the dragon can free me from my endless labor, but
he takes no pity on me."

As Henry stepped from the ferry, he offered to
speak to the dragon, and the fisherman promised him
a great reward.

Leaving the river behind, the woodcutter's son
entered the forest and began climbing a steep path.
Soon he saw the walls of the dragon's palace glittering
before him.

Henry stepped forward boldly, knocked at the gate, and was greeted by the dragon's wife, for the dragon was not at home. Now, though the dragon was fearsome, his wife never harmed anyone.

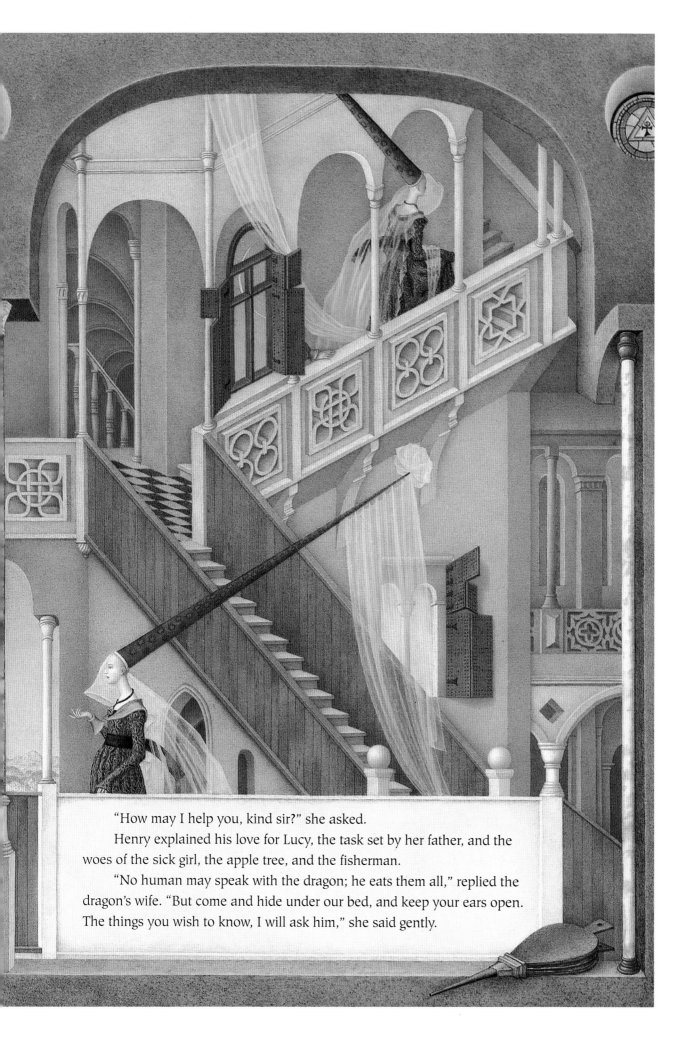

"How may I help you, kind sir?" she asked.

Henry explained his love for Lucy, the task set by her father, and the woes of the sick girl, the apple tree, and the fisherman.

"No human may speak with the dragon; he eats them all," replied the dragon's wife. "But come and hide under our bed, and keep your ears open. The things you wish to know, I will ask him," she said gently.

Late, late that night the dragon returned home. As soon as he entered
the palace, he stretched out his neck, peered all around, sniffed the air,
and roared, "I smell . . . I smell . . . a woodcutter's son."
"No, no, my dear," replied the dragon's wife, stroking his feathers and gazing up
at him. "No one has been here all day." The dragon slowly calmed down, and
as his wife murmured flattering words to him, he grew silent and contented.

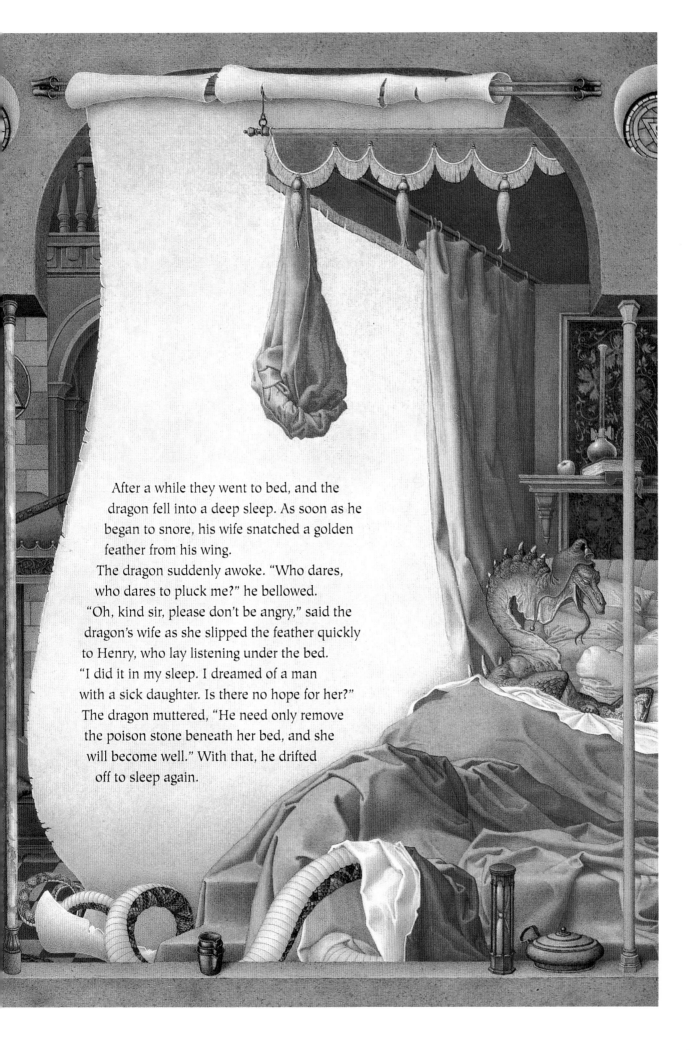

After a while they went to bed, and the
dragon fell into a deep sleep. As soon as he
began to snore, his wife snatched a golden
feather from his wing.

The dragon suddenly awoke. "Who dares,
who dares to pluck me?" he bellowed.

"Oh, kind sir, please don't be angry," said the
dragon's wife as she slipped the feather quickly
to Henry, who lay listening under the bed.
"I did it in my sleep. I dreamed of a man
with a sick daughter. Is there no hope for her?"
The dragon muttered, "He need only remove
the poison stone beneath her bed, and she
will become well." With that, he drifted
off to sleep again.

As soon as the dragon began to snore, his wife pulled out another feather and handed it to Henry.

"Who dares, who dares to pluck me?" roared the dragon.

"Lie still, my sweet husband. I had a dream about a tree that no longer bears golden apples. If only I knew how it might become fruitful again, I could sleep peacefully."

"A snake lies under the tree devouring the roots. It must be dug out and killed," said the dragon, and soon dropped off to sleep again.

Swiftly, the wife snatched out the third golden feather and dropped it to Henry. The dragon sat up in a rage, ready to spring from the bed. "Who dares, who dares to pluck me?" he screeched in a terrible high voice.

But his wife held him tight in her arms and said,
"Quiet, quiet, my dear. I dreamed of a fisherman who must
forever pole a ferry across a broad river."
"The silly fool may give the job to the first person who comes
to him, then run away a free man," the dragon snorted.
"Now, leave me in peace!"
As the dragon fell asleep, Henry crawled silently from
his hiding place, whispered his thanks to the dragon's wife,
and crept out of the castle.

Setting out for home, Henry soon reached
the ferry. The fisherman asked him hopefully
for news from the dragon. "Please take me
across the river first," said Henry.

As soon as they bumped against the far bank, Henry told the fisherman, "The next time someone comes along, put the pole in his hands, and he must take your place forever." So happy was the fisherman that he gave Henry all his money.

Henry made his way back to where the people stood around the barren apple tree. As soon as he told them of the snake, they dug it out and killed it, and immediately the tree began to bud and bear golden fruit again. The people were so joyous that they loaded Henry with gold and silver.

Upon reaching the farmer's cottage, Henry told him the dragon's words. When the man removed the poison stone, his daughter leapt from the bed with the bloom of health in her cheeks. The delighted father sent Henry on his way with a thousand thanks and a bag of coins.

Happiest of all was Lucy when she saw her dear Henry again. She gazed into her beloved's eyes as he told her his story, then took him by the hand to see her father. Henry gave the innkeeper the three golden feathers, and since the woodcutter's son was now far richer than he himself, Lucy's father agreed to their marriage.

"Where in the world did you get all this money?" asked the innkeeper.

"From the dragon in the dark forest," replied Henry. "The easiest way to get there is to take the ferry."

The innkeeper set out at once, but strange to say, he was never heard from again.

Henry and Lucy invited all the people of the village to their wedding party in the courtyard of the inn. Everyone feasted and danced, but the young lovers danced longest into the night.

Meshack Asare

CAT
IN SEARCH OF A FRIEND

KM Kane/Miller Book Publishers

Cat in Search of a Friend

WRITTEN AND ILLUSTRATED BY MESHACK ASARE

Do you want to be my friend?" asks Cat, the main character in this starkly illustrated African story. Cat not only wants a friend, she wants a protector, so she seeks the strongest animal in the jungle. From a monkey to an elephant, each animal the cat befriends is succeeded by a stronger one. A seemingly simple tale, *Cat in Search of a Friend* actually gives us wonderful insight into the different creatures that roam Africa. A deeper message about human behavior is conveyed, but like many of Asare's stories, it is voiced by an animal.

Meshack Asare's moody illustrations are inspired by African art. Through the use of earth tones and loose watercolor, he brings us into the heart of the African wilderness. He uses white backgrounds as backdrops to accentuate the animals, making them seem sharper and bolder.

A renowned artist, Asare is one of the first African illustrators to break through to European and American markets. Born in 1945 in central Ghana, he studied art at the University of Science and Technology in Kumasi and then taught at two American schools in Ghana for twelve years.

In 1970, inspired by his work as a teacher, Asare began writing and illustrating children's books. His first work, *Tawia Goes to the Sea,* was selected as the Best African Book of 1970 by UNESCO. Ten years and several books later, *The Brassman's Secret* won the Noma Award in 1982 as the best book produced in Africa. Growing international recognition of Asare's ability as a writer and artist led to his first full-color book, *Cat in Search of a Friend,* which one German expert praised as "an artistic achievement which draws from the artist's own cultural and social roots." Today Meshack Asare continues to illustrate books and sculpts. He currently lives in London.

Once upon a time there was a cat who had yellow fur. She also had a bushy yellow tail and eyes the color of honey.

One thing she didn't have, however, was a friend with whom she could stay and who would protect her. And that made her sad.

One day she went to the little monkeys and asked them,

"Do you want to be my friend?"

"Why not?" answered the little monkeys. "You will never find better and stronger friends than us."

So the cat with the yellow fur stayed with the monkeys and played with them until . . . the chimpanzees came.

Suddenly the little monkeys were afraid and ran away.

"The chimpanzees are even stronger than the little monkeys," said the cat with the yellow fur to herself. "So they will be better friends."

And she stayed with the chimpanzees and played with them.

Until . . . the gorillas came.

When the chimpanzees saw the
gorillas, they ran away.

Until . . . the leopard came.
When it became night and was very
dark, the leopard crept on soft paws. Then
the gorillas vanished, not to be seen again.

"The gorillas are even stronger than the chimpanzees," said the cat with the yellow fur to herself. "They are the right friends for me."

And she stayed with the gorillas and played with them.

"Just as I thought," said the cat with the yellow fur to herself. "The strongest is naturally the one who looks like me, only with spots and bigger."

And she took the leopard as her friend and did not leave its side.

Until . . . the rhinoceros came and wanted to drink at the same water hole as the lion.

The lion gave up its place without even being asked.

Until . . . the lion came along
and gave out a ferocious roar.

Then the leopard vanished.

"Aha," said the cat with the yellow fur to
herself. "Creatures like us need only a bushy
mane to lord over others."

And she took the lion as a friend and did
not leave its side.

"That's it!" said the cat with the yellow fur to herself. "A horn on the nose—it's not beautiful, but it is useful."

And she took the rhino as a friend and did not leave its side.

Until . . . the elephant came.

The elephant was even bigger than the rhinoceros. Certainly it must also be much stronger. The earth trembled under its steps.

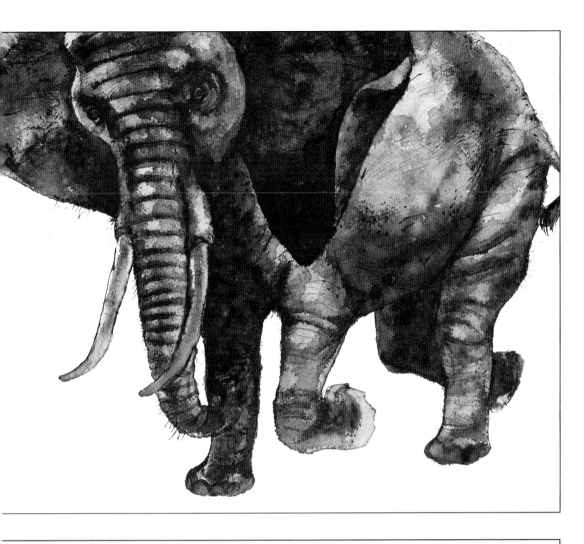

"There it is!" said the cat with the yellow fur to herself. "One must have a trunk and tusks, not just a horn on the nose."

And she took the elephant as her friend and did not leave its side.

When the man turned his back, the elephant quickly got to its feet and lumbered away.

"Aha," said the cat with the yellow fur to herself. "This time the elephant got away, but if someone walks on two legs and carries a gun, then he must be very strong indeed."

Suddenly the elephant crashed to the ground.
"What's the matter with you big strong elephant?" asked the cat with the yellow fur. "Why do you just lie there without moving?"
"Sh-h-h," said the elephant. "Don't you see the man with the gun? I want him to think that I'm dead."

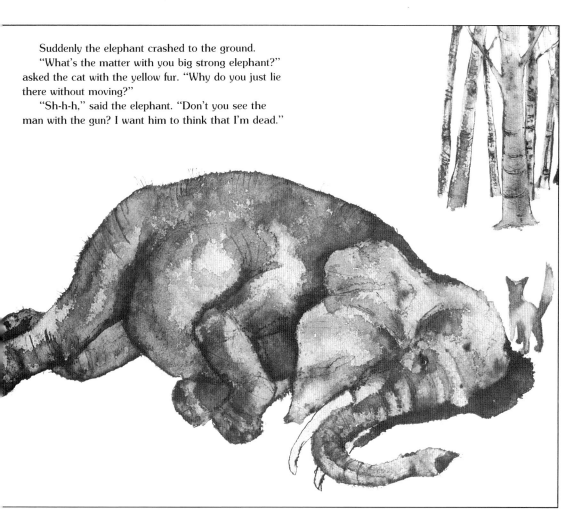

And she made the man her master and friend and didn't leave his side.

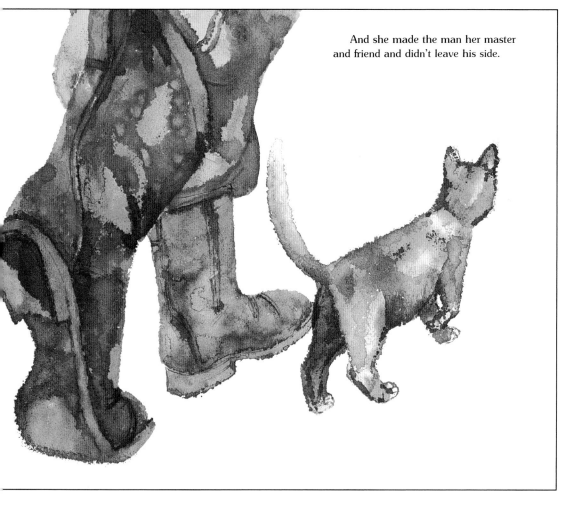

"Look," said the cat with the yellow fur to herself. "It was a good thing I didn't decide right away to stay forever with the man. The woman is stronger than the strongest man. From now on the woman shall be my master.

And she stayed with her.

Until . . . the man came to his hut.

"Again you didn't shoot any animal for our food," scolded the man's wife, and she ran after him with a wooden spoon.

But when a mouse ran across the room, the woman jumped up on a chair and screamed for help.

The cat only said, "Pffff!" and the mouse disappeared.

"Look now," said the cat with the yellow fur to herself. "In the end there's really no one stronger than I."

"My friend can be anybody,
I alone am my own master."

افسانهٔ درخت خرما و بزی

بازآفرینی از افسانهٔ منظوم درخت آسوریگ : محمّد محمّدی

نقاشی : سارا ایروانی

The Legend of the Palm Tree and the Goat (Afsaneh Derakhteh Khorma Va Bozi)

WRITTEN BY MOHAMMAD MOHAMMADI

TRANSLATED BY HOURA YAVARI

ILLUSTRATED BY SARA IRAVANI

The Legend of the Palm Tree and the Goat is based on a pre-Islamic tale about what might seem to be a battle of wits between a palm tree and a goat. In fact, it represents a symbolic confrontation between the era of agriculture, as represented by the tree, and the era of herdmanship, as represented by the goat—a struggle between two ways of life that has been central to Iran's history. It also serves as a tribute to the country's historic roots in children's literature.

Originally written in the Pahlavi language (spoken in what is today Iran between the third and seventh centuries A.D.), the text was later translated into Persian by Dr. Mahyar Navabi. Mohammad Mohammadi shaped it into rhythmic verse so it could be acted out as a play for young readers. The original Pahlavi script appears in the background art, which serves as a reminder of the legend's past.

Using the combined mediums of water-color, acrylic, gouache, and colored pencils, Sara Iravani has created an elaborate traditional style for this ancient tale. She has incorporated motifs that have adorned pottery from the pre-Islamic period, thus hinting at the country's rich symbolic life. For example, on page 128, the twelve goats circling the earth symbolize the twelve months of the year. The use of contrasting colors of vermilion and turquoise echoes their prominence in ancient manuscripts and reinforces the conflict between the tree and the goat.

Mohammad Mohammadi was born in Tehran, Iran, in 1961. His first work was published in 1989, and he has since written sixteen books for children and young adults. Sara Iravani was born in the United States in 1965 and has five books to her credit. She has won awards at both national and international exhibitions in Iran, and her works have been exhibited at Bologna and Bratislava. Both the author and illustrator currently live in Tehran.

بازآفرینی از افسانه کهن درخت آسوریگ :   م ـ محمدی

درخت خرما و بزی طرح جدیدی است از افسانه کهن درخت آسوریگ. اصل این افسانه به زبان پهلوی، یکی از زبانهای کهن ایرانی، است. درخت آسوریگ افسانه‌ای منظوم است که بیانگر اندیشه و باور ایرانیان و همسایگانشان در روزگاران دور است. همچنین این افسانه شیرین به ما یادآوری می‌کند که ادبیات کودکان مکتوب چه ریشه کهنی در این مرز و بوم دارد . دکتر ماهیار نوابی این افسانه را به فارسی برگردانده است و من با استفاده از برگردان ایشان آن را باز آفرینی کرده‌ام. زبان درخت خرما و بزی نثر آهنگین است. این افسانه قابلیت زیادی برای اجرای نمایشی در مهد کودکها و مدرسه‌ها دارد.

There was a river called the Euphrates,
Its water sweeter than all honeys.
Along this pure river,
Trees sprouted everywhere,
Trees green as spring,
Willows and plane trees
With umbrellas tufted above their heads
Where nightingales and storks made their nests.
They had branches, like shining grapes,
Burning like chandeliers.

But there was one tree, quite tall,
With the hardest wood of all,
Shouting out: Here I am, here I am.
Here I am—the great heroic palm.
Here I am—strongest and most robust.
Here I am—tall as a ladder and young.
Here I am—full of life and strong.
Is there anybody, wise and bright,
Who dares to come close and fight?

بزی بود بلا

با شاخ سیاه

با دم کوتاه

ریش حنا

خوش و با صفا

تنهای تنها

تشنه که شد

دوید و دوید

به ساحل فرات رسید.

همینکه سر به آب رساند

به آب پاک پاک رساند

عکس غولی کاکل به سر

می‌جنبید و بلند می‌خواند

حالا کی می‌آید به جنگم؟

تا من با او بجنگم؟

And there was a goat, a clever one,
A goat with black horns and a short tail,
A goat with a henna-dyed beard,
A jolly goat, just by himself,
All alone but happy with himself.

One day, the little goat was thirsty.
He scurried all over searching for water.
He ran and ran, here and there.

He reached the Euphrates River
With crystal water so pure and clear.
He dipped his head into the river.
Lo and behold, a beast was in the water,
A moving beast, with a tufted umbrella,
Shouting out:
I am dying for a fight,
Are you ready to fight?

بز شاخ سیاه

با دم کوتاه

این حرف را شنید

عقب کشید

شاخ کشید

به من می‌گویند، بزک بلا

خیلی ناقلا

پهلوانم، اهل جنگ

شکست باشد برایم ننگ

شاخهایم سخت تر از سنگ

با همه شوم چنگ در چنگ

حالا کی می‌آید با من جنگ؟

خرما می‌زد به طبل جنگ

دنگ، دنگ، دنگ

دنگ، دنگ، دنگ

نام من خرما

سر من هوا

میوه‌ام از طلا

The goat with black horns,
The goat with the short tail
Was angry at what he heard.
He moved back and said:
People call me the goat,
The clever goat, who is very smart,

The goat who is always ready to fight.
With his horns as hard as rocks,
He gives a lesson to those who dare fight.
Now, it is I who am dying for a fight.
Are you ready to test my might?

The palm tree struck his drum,
Dum, dum, dum,
Dum, dum, dum,
I am the palm.

With my head high and calm,
My fruits are like gold,
That is the way it is told.
With my leaves big and green,
I look better than spring.

We make a garden, my friends and I.
They all come to us and say hi.
The priest, the sage, the young and the old
Love my dates that gleam like gold.

Oh, dear little goat
With twisted horns!
People use my hard wood
To make timber for their boats.
People sweep their rooms
With my leaves, woven into brooms.
They use my round trunk,
My big, hard trunk,
To pound the rice and grind the wheat
In big, round mortars,
Thump, thump, thump,
For making food so they can eat.

بزک بلا
خیلی ناقلا
از چوب من
من کهن
از برگ تن
از شاخه‌هایم چون آهن

پاپوش سازند
پاپوش تخت
برای راه سخت سخت
طناب بافند
طناب سفت
گره زنند مانند چفت

از تن من چوب تراشند
چوب کتک
برای مثل تو بزک
چوب کتک که پشت و پیشت بزنند
به دم و ریشت بزنند!

بزیزی جان
آوازه خوان
آدم گاهی چوب مرا تیز می‌کند
سیخ می‌کند
سیخ مرا دار می‌کند
دار پای بار می‌کند

بار آتش
آتش و دود
سرخ و کبود
گوشتت را رشته می‌کند
سرخ و برشته می‌کند

I burn in fireplaces, I make
Hot and glistening flames.
I feed furnaces
For the old ironsmith
Who snores in his sleep.

Oh, clever little goat,
Very cunning goat!
They use my wood and my leaves,

My branches and twigs,
To make shoes and other things,
To weave ropes so strong
They will never break apart.

My wood is carved into sticks
To beat the likes of you sick,
To beat them on their tail and
   to beat them on their crown.

Oh, dear little goat,
My precious singing goat!
They take my branches
To make pointed sticks
And use them as grill spits.
They make fire to grill
Your crimson flesh, until
The flames, maroon and red,
Bake your strips, so it is said!

بز شاخ سیاه

با دم کوتاه

تابستانها با سایه‌ام

به مثل سقف خانه‌ام

خانه برای اسب و شیر

سایهٔ سر مرد فقیر

بز ریش حنا

خوش و باصفا

شهد من هست خیلی شیرین

از روزگار دیرین

از آغاز فروردین

از شهد من شربت کنند

شربت خوب و خوشمزه

تو هم بنوش ، مزه مزه!

بزک کوچک

تنها و تک

از برگهای درازم

Oh, you black-horned goat,
Goat with a short tail!
With my shade in the summer
Spreading everywhere,
I make a roof, here and there,
For the lion, for the horse, and for the horseman,
For the young and for the poor old man.

Oh, jolly and merry goat,
Goat with the henna-tinged beard!
Since old, very old days, it is said,
People have always made
Sherbets that are the tastiest
With my nectar, which is the sweetest.
Would you like to join and have a taste?

باکاکلهای نازم
کیسه و گونی می‌بافند
کیسه برای همه چیز
برای آلو و مویز
کیسه دارو و شکر
کیسه زردچوبه و پَر

بزک بلا خیال نکن همین است وبس
چیزهای دیگر هم هست
هان، هان، هان !
میان کاکل من
افشان مثل موی زن

جای پرنده‌ها هست
لانهٔ مرغ ماهیخوار
گنجشک با طوطی و سار
بزک بلا
شاد و خوش آوا

حالا تو دیدی خرما
خرمای خوب و زیبا
با آن قامت رعنا
چقدر هست او توانا؟
یادت باشد هرکه بکارد هسته‌ام
این هستهٔ سر بسته‌ام

شوم درختی پر میوه
نگو به من عمو دیوه
میوه‌ام شیرین
مثل نگین
رنگ طلا
خرما! خرما!

Oh, my little goat,
My little lonely goat!
They make pouches and bags
With my long leaves and tufts,
Sacks for everything,
For raisins and plums,
For drugs and sugar,
For spice and feathers.

Oh, my little goat,
My little clever goat!
Don't think the tale is over.
There is much, much more.

Seagulls and sparrows,
Starlings and parrots
Build their nests among my
    tufted leaves,
Which flow like waves in the sea
And look like hair you would
    love to see.

Oh, my clever goat,
My merry and enchanting goat!
Do you know me now,
The heroic palm,
The tallest of them all,

The most graceful and the
    strongest?
Have you ever heard of my
    seeds,
My mysterious little seeds,
Which will grow into trees
Rich with fruits, and lush with
    leaves?
My leaves are the greenest,
My fruits the sweetest
My golden fruit, the date,
The sweet date, fit for a feast.
Don't you dare call me a beast!

Now it was the goat's turn,
The goat with the short tail,
To strike the drum,
dum, dum, dum,
dum, dum, dum.

Do you hear me, you tall beast?
Here I am, the one who leads,
The one who sings with the shepherds

When they play their pipes for their herds:
Maa, maa, maa,
Maa, maa, maa.

I have milk, cream, and cheese,
Which taste so good with sweet cakes.
Both teachers and learned men
Eat them along with poor men.

کنار چشمه‌های آب
یا که با موی زبر من
کمر بافند روپیراهن
کمر با دانه مروارید
که می‌تابد مثل خورشید
از پوست من

عمو دیو دراز
گردن، فراز
موهای زبر تن من
دامن شود بر تن زن
پوشش شود بر سر و تن
سیاه چادر برای خواب

چین وشکن
با نخ و سوزن
چکمه‌دوزندخیلی‌قشنگ
دستکش‌هایگرم‌وخوش‌رنگ
برای مرد و زن پیر
برای دهقان و وزیر

نامه برای یار کنند
تومار برای صد پند
نامه به دوست دلبند

عمو دیو دراز
سایه‌ات پر راز

یا که شوم مشکه آب
زیر آفتاب
برای تشنهٔ بی‌تاب
هم می‌شوم سفره ناب
بچین در آن مرغ وکباب
از پوست من تومار کنند

Oh, great tall beast
With the long neck!
The people use my rough hair
To make clothes to wear.
They also make tents
  with my hair
In which they can rest
  here and there.
They weave belts with my hair,
Belts decorated with
  sparkling pearls,

Belts they put over
  what they wear.
The people work with their
  needles and threads
On my skin, on my rough skin,
To make pleated boots
  and warm gloves
For peasants and for old men,
For priests and for old women,
Or they make leather jugs
For the thirsty to fill their mugs.

I can also be a tablecloth,
  soft and nice,
Good for setting out chicken,
  kabob, and rice.
The people make scrolls
  out of my leather,
Which is the best for
  writing a letter,
A letter to a friend,
  to give some advice,
To a sweetheart, lovely and nice.

موی تنم

پارچه نرم

شالهای گرم

پارچه برای پیراهن

شال برای پیرزن

کیسه پیکان

چرمینه ریسمان

در دست صد پهلوان

پهلوانان نامدار

در میدان کارزار

از روده‌ام، پوست تنم

که من، منم

بر تو سرم

چه‌ها سازند!

زه کمان

عمو دیو دراز

بزن تو به ساز

تا بزی بخواند آواز

با چرم بز کیسه کنند

کیسه آرد، انار و پنیر

Oh, great tall beast!
Play on your flute
So I can sing you a nice tune.
My wool makes soft fabric,
Good for dresses and fine shawls
To keep old women wrapped up and warm.

My skin and my gut
Make the best bowstrings,
Leather sacks for bows,
And strong ropes for heroes
To win the wars, to trap the foes.

عطر و شکر، فلفل و سیر

کلاه و کفش، مشکهٔ شیر

بازرگانها شهر به شهر

کوه به کوه

گروه گروه

از کشور ایران‌زمین

که هر جایش باشد نگین

تا هند و چین

با من روند

با کیسه‌ها از پوست من

با کیسه‌ها از موی تن

موی سفیدم نرم نرم

پیراهنهای گرم گرم

پیراهن کوچک، بزرگ

گاهی به رنگ پوست گرگ

دامنهای یک‌چین دوچین

تا بازارهای هند و چین

خرما جانم

من که بزم

خیلی خوشم

هر روز می‌روم به یک سو

یک روز به جنگل و کوه

یک روز به دشت خوشبو

یک روز به پیش آهو

یک روز به ساحل دور

Oh, great tall beast!
I want to sing more songs, old and new,
So you will know what I can do.
People make sacks with my leather,
Sacks for pomegranates, flour, and sugar,
Sacks for garlic, perfumes, and pepper,
Sacks for hats, sacks for shoes, all from leather.

Merchants carry the sacks
From town to town,

From mountain to mountain,
From the land of Persia,
Which shines like a gem,
To China and to India.
They carry the sacks made of my skin,
They carry the sacks made of my wool,
My soft, fine, white wool,
Filled with warm gowns, small and large,
Filled with fluffy skirts, from Persia, to India,
    to China.

یک روز به باغ انگور

هر جا آدم به یک رنگ

گاهی با چشمان تنگ

گاهی پوست سیاه رنگ

در جنگل و کوه سنگ

از شیر من می‌دوشند

با عسلش می‌نوشند

از گوشت من پزند غذا

عطرش همیشه در هوا

از پوست من سازند چه‌ها

تومار برای داستان

جلد برای قلمدان

تنبک تنبور، بزن تو آسان!

Oh, my dear palm tree!
I am a goat, a jolly goat.
Each day, I take one direction—
One day to forests, one day to mountains,
One day to the fragrances of the low plains,
One day to distant seashores,
One day to vineyards,
One day to spend with lovely deers.

Wherever I go, I see people,
People in different colors,
People with different faces,
Who love to drink my milk
And cook my meat to make a nice meal,
Filling the air with its scent.
Many things they make of my skin,
Scrolls for stories and covers for pens
And, look, drums for you to play!

When they take me to the market,
They yell, "Here we have a nice goat
Whose meat is sweet like custard,
Whose milk is filling like a meal,
With the prettiest wool,
With a black horn,
With a henna-dyed beard,

Worth his weight in gold."
But who is going to pay
One penny to buy you one day?
Palm trees grow everywhere,
Like grains of sand, here and there.
Dates are very cheap, now and ever,
Like grains of sand on beaches everywhere.

من که بزم به کوه روم
کوهی نوکش برف سفید
که می تابد بر آن خورشید
از این طرف به آن طرف
تا دشت خوشبو از علف

I can climb mountains, fast and slow,
Mountains covered with ice and snow.
I can run with the bright shining sun
From this side to the other one,
To fresh-scented prairies.

اما تو چه؟

مثل یک میخ

یا که یک سیخ

چسبیده‌ای بر خاک نرم

در ساحلهای خیلی گرم

حالا دیدی خرما جان

این بزی هست قهرمان

خرما شد خیلی گریان

همین طوری ماند حیران

فهمید که بز برنده است

شاد با لب پر خنده است

بز خندان

پوستش گران

شاخش کمان

سفید دندان

دوید و دوید

تا به طویله‌اش رسید

رفت خانه‌اش قرص خورشید

ستاره‌ای از راه رسید

با مهتاب آبی سفید

بزک روی علف لمید

خمیازه‌ای با ناز کشید

خوب و خوش و راحت خوابید

این افسانه به سر رسید.

But what about you,
Grown and nailed
   to the soft ground
Or on hot seashores,
   stuck and bound?
Now, you see, my dear one?
It is the goat who has won.

The palm tree was crying.
He could not believe his ears.

He knew the goat had won
With a smile spread
   from ear to ear.

The smiling goat
With the expensive wool,
With the black horn
And white bright teeth,
Ran and ran
To reach his barn,

Which was shining like the sun.
Then the moon came and night
With its stars, sparkling
   and bright.
The goat slept on the lawn
With a lazy yawn,
Slept a deep and peaceful one
And left us this tale,
   so nice and fun.

The Legend of the Palm Tree and the Goat 129

חָמֵשׁ מְכַשְׁפוֹת הָלְכוּ לְטַיֵּל

כָּתְבָה: רוֹנִית חָכָם

אִיְּרָה: אוֹרְנָה אִיַּל

Five Wacky Witches (Hamesh Mechashefot Halchu Letayel)

WRITTEN BY RONIT CHACHAM

TRANSLATED BY DORON NARKISS AND RONIT CHACHAM

ILLUSTRATED BY ORA AYAL

Legend has it that Ora Ayal and Ronit Chacham, who have been working together for many years, were walking along the streets of Jerusalem one day when they bumped into a group of strange-looking women. The women seemed to be enjoying themselves immensely, giggling, singing, and carrying on—just like five wacky witches. Ora and Ronit decided to follow the five women, and they based a children's book on the women's escapade.

Whether their story is believable or not, the book *Five Wacky Witches* is certainly entertaining. The 1995 Israel Museum Ben Yitzak Award for Outstanding Children's Book Illustration went to Ora Ayal, whose colorful characters and fantastical surroundings seem to spring directly from Ronit Chacham's whimsical rhymed story. This literary spectacle makes the idea of a witches' day on the town seem like an occurrence anyone would love to have seen firsthand.

Ora Ayal was born and raised in Jerusalem, Israel. She studied graphic design at the Bezalel Academy of Arts and graduated from the Hebrew University with a degree in mathematics. She has written and illustrated more than sixty children's books, many of them award winning. She has also collaborated in the development of stories and games to be used for teaching math to young children.

Ronit Chacham was also born in Israel, where she studied English literature and philosophy at the Hebrew University. She has worked in children's theater and has written children's books, educational programs, and novels. Currently, she is coeditor of *News from Within,* a Jewish-Palestinian monthly publication.

Both Ronit Chacham and Ora Ayal currently live and work in Jerusalem. As for the five wacky witches, no recent sightings have been reported.

חָמֵשׁ מְכַשֵּׁפוֹת הָלְכוּ לְטַיֵּל,   אוֹהוּ, אוֹהוֹ

הָלְכוּ קְצָת בַּשֶּׁמֶשׁ, הָלְכוּ קְצָת בַּצֵּל,   אוֹהוּ, אוֹהָא.

הֵן הָיוּ מְאֹד עַלִּיזוֹת וּשְׂמֵחוֹת,   צָנוֹן וָלֶפֶת

וְשָׁרוּ שִׁירִים בְּקוֹל יַנְשׁוּפוֹת: רַגְלֵי קַרְפָּדָה.

Five wacky witches went walking along.
On high roads and byroads, they roared out a song.
With rickety fingers and boils on their toes,
They hopped and they croaked like a band of hoarse toads:

    Pradeep, pradeep,
    Pradeep, pradoo.
    Slugs and bugs,
    And how do you do.

Five wacky witches
    caught a bus into town.
When they got to the station,
    they marched up and down.
They wanted to look
    at the crowds passing by,
So they climbed up a house that
    was five stories high.

They ate some fruit,
    an orange or so,
And threw the peels

on the people below.
They giggled and fiddled
    and played funny games,
Then ran down the street
    calling out naughty names.

But—
One witch bumped into a pole,
Where she got tangled up
    and couldn't let go.
She cried, "Girls, help me!" and
begged them to stay,

But none of them heard her,
    they were too far away.
With rickety fingers
    and boils on their toes,
They hopped and they croaked
    like a band of hoarse toads:

Pradeep, pradeep,
Pradeep, pradoo.
Slugs and bugs
And how do you do.

Four wacky witches went
   wheeling and dealing,
Walked into a store
   and danced on the ceiling.
They tried on some hats,
   pink knickers, and gloves,
They dressed up like ladies
   with glasses and scarves.

They rode on the broomsticks,
   made all the shoes squeak,

In and out of the mirrors they
   played hide-and-seek.
When they left, they twirled the
   doors around and about,
Then they ran away laughing and
   gave a great shout.

But—
One wacky witch got stuck
   on a stair.

She called, "Girls, wait for me!"
   but *they* didn't care.
With rickety fingers
   and boils on their toes,
They hopped and they croaked
   like a band of hoarse toads:

Pradeep, pradeep,
Pradeep, pradoo.
Slugs and bugs
And how do you do.

Three wacky witches
at a fancy café
Had chocolate-chip cookies
   and cakes on a tray.
They talked very loudly
   and told stupid jokes,
They hiccuped and lizards
   jumped out of their throats.

The lizards took baths in the
   cups and the plates
And jumped on the table
   and gobbled the cakes.

The waiter got frightened,
   his hair stood on end.
He dropped a cream pie on a
   customer's head.

The witches laughed so,
   their cheeks got all sore.
They fell off their chairs
   and rolled on the floor.
Then they tied up the lizards
   and tickled their feet
And tittered and cackled
   away down the street.

But—
One of the witches fell into a pie.
She cried, "Help me, you witches!"
   but they didn't try.
With rickety fingers and boils on
   their toes,
They hopped and they croaked
   like a band of hoarse toads:

Pradeep, pradeep,
Pradeep, pradoo.
Slugs and bugs
And how do you do.

Two wacky witches
   walking at ease
Came to a store
   that was selling TVs.
They were showing a movie
   that was terribly scary
With the monster Asmodeus,
   all horribly hairy.

The witches loved movies,
   it was not what *they* feared,

But then what came up
   was incredibly weird.
Asmodeus looked at the witches
   with greed:
"Come here, little witchy-poo,
   you're just what I need!"

He lit a great fire, stuck his arms
   through the screen,
Grabbed one of the witches,
   and pulled her right in.

He put her straight into a huge
   copper pot
And said to his son,
   "Come 'n' eat while it's hot!"

Pradeep, pradeep,
Pradeep, pradoo.
Stew of worms
And a witchy-poo too.

הַיֶּלֶד הִמְשִׁיךְ לְהַבִּיט לְאָחוֹר
הַמְּכַשֵּׁפָה עָשְׂתָה לוֹ פַּרְצוּף שֶׁל חֲמוֹר.
הִיא הָיְתָה מְאֹד עַלִּיזָה וּשְׂמֵחָה
וְשָׁרָה שִׁירִים בְּקוֹל יְנָשׁוּפָה:

אוֹהוּ, אוֹהוּ
אוֹהוּ, אוֹהָא.
צְנוֹן וָלֶפֶת
רַגְלֵי קַרְפָּדָה.

One wacky witch alone and quite dumb.
A little boy saw her and said to his mom,
"I see a witch, Mommy, do you think
    she likes boys?"
His mother said, "Darling, don't make
    so much noise.
And besides, there is no such thing, my pet.
Now, come along nicely, Mommy's terribly late!"

מְכַשֵּׁפָה אַחַת נִשְׁאֲרָה לְבַדָּהּ,
רָאָה אוֹתָהּ יֶלֶד קָטָן וְקָרָא:
"אִמָּא, תִּרְאִי, הִנֵּה מְכַשֵּׁפָה!"
אַךְ אִמּוֹ אָחֲזָה בְּיָדוֹ וְאָמְרָה:
"אֵין בָּעוֹלָם מְכַשֵּׁפוֹת, חֲמוּדִי,
בּוֹא נֵלֵךְ, אֲנִי מְמַהֶרֶת נוֹרָא!"

The boy kept turning his head back to stare.
The witch pulled a face like a stupid old mare.
With rickety fingers and boils on her toes,
She hopped and she croaked
   like a very hoarse toad:

   Pradeep, pradeep,
   Pradeep, pradoo.
   Slugs and bugs
   And how do you do.

One wacky witch went on
  with the trip.
She climbed up a tower
  and sat on the tip.
She looked at the view
  but felt all alone.
It made her upset
  to be on her own.

She pulled out a broomstick,
  which she kept just in case,
And to the TV store she rode with
  great haste.

She scattered some witch dust
  and conjured a charm,
Asmodeus sh-shivvvverred
  in fear and alarm.

The witch in the pot
  jumped out with a shout,
Cursing and kicking
  and spitting about.
Her friend simply said,
  "Now, do as you're told:
Shut up and get on,
  or else you'll catch cold."

She quickly shut up, combed
  her hair, blew her nose,
Freshened her makeup,
  and corrected her pose.
Two witches now sat on the
  broomstick and rode
And croaked out their song
  like a band of hoarse toads:

Pradeep, pradeep,
Pradeep, pradoo.
Slugs and bugs
And how do you do.

Two witches sat on the
  broomstick and sped.
To the fancy café with
  the lizards they fled.
They found a poor witch
  in a squashy cream pie
With cherries on top
  and some jam in her eye.

With her hands on her hips, she
  whined and she moaned,

"While you had a party,
  I was left here alone!"
The witches just said,
  "Now, do as you're told:
Shut up and get on,
  or else you'll catch cold!"

She quickly shut up,
  combed her hair, blew her nose,
Powdered her cheeks,
  and corrected her pose.

Three witches now sat on the
  broomstick and rode
And croaked out their song
  like a band of hoarse toads:

Pradeep, pradeep,
Pradeep, pradoo.
Slugs and bugs
And how do you do.

Three witches stopped with a
  screech at the store
Where their friend was still stuck
  in a stair by the door.
The dress she had on was all
  matted, in creases,
She'd grown a mustache,
  and her nose was in pieces!

With her hands on her hips, she
  whined and she moaned,

"While you had your fun, I was
  stuck here alone!"
The witches just said,
  "Now, do as you're told:
Shut up and get on,
  or else you'll catch cold!"

She quickly shut up,
  combed her hair, fixed her nose,
Straightened her dress, and
  corrected her pose.

Four witches now sat on the
  broomstick and rode
And croaked out their song
  like a band of hoarse toads:

Pradeep, pradeep,
Pradeep, pradoo.
Slugs and bugs
And how do you do.

Four witches flew on the broom
  at great pace,
Parked by a house where they
  soon found a space.
From the roof, their friend shouted,
  "You witches don't care!
Birds have already built
  a nest in my hair!"

With her hands on her hips, she
  whined and she moaned,

"While you went out shopping,
  I hung here alone!"
The witches just said,
  "Now, do as you're told:
Shut up and get on,
  or else you'll catch cold!"

She quickly jumped down,
  combed her hair, blew her nose,
Looked in the mirror, and
  corrected her pose.

Five witches now sat on the
  broomstick and rode
And croaked out their song
  like a band of hoarse toads:

Pradeep, pradeep,
Pradeep, pradoo.
Slugs and bugs
And how do you do.

Five wacky witches flew happily home,
Picking their noses and feeling all warm.
They clashed the pots and pans with a bang,
Brewed a big broth, and round it they sang:

Pradeep, pradeep,
Pradeep, pradoo.
Crocodile soup
And a smelly old shoe.

חָמֵשׁ מְכַשְׁפוֹת מְאוֹד הִתְעַיְּפוּ,
סָרְקוּ שְׂעָרָן, פִּיגָ׳מוֹת לָבְשׁוּ,
נִכְנְסוּ לַמִּטּוֹת, הִתְכַּסּוּ בִּשְׂמִיכוֹת,
עָצְמוּ עֵינֵיהֶן וְחָלְמוּ חֲלוֹמוֹת:

אוֹהוֹוֹוֹוֹוֹוֹ, אוֹהוֹוֹוֹוֹוֹוֹ
אוֹהוֹוֹוֹוֹוֹוֹ, אוֹהָהָהָהָהָא,
צְצְצָצְנוּן וַלְלְלֶלֶפֶת
רַגְלְלְלְלְלֵי עַכְכְכְכְכַּבָּרָרָהָהָהָהָהָהָהָהָהָהָהּ.

Five wacky witches at the end of their treat
Felt so very tired they fell off their feet.
They took off their socks and got into bed
Pulled up the covers, lay head next to head.
Swiftly came sleep and swept them away
To dream
    of the fun
       they had that day.

Pradeeeeep, pradeeeeep,
Pradeeeeep, pradoooooo.
Sliiimy sluuuugs
Are
    dreeeaaming
       of yoooooooooou.

PAIKEA

Robyn Kahukiwa

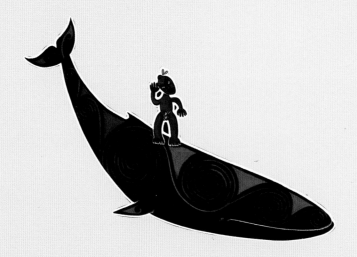

Paikea

WRITTEN AND ILLUSTRATED BY ROBYN KAHUKIWA

Located deep in the South Pacific, New Zealand is a country rich in ancient and mystical history. *Paikea* is just one example of its magnificent legends. In Maori and Polynesian mythology, Paikea is a well-known *tipuna*, or ancestor, of the indigenous Maori people of New Zealand, most of whom live on the east coast of North Island. Now, Paikea's journey across the ocean *Te Moana-nui a Kiwa* (the Pacific) from Hawaiki to Aotearoa (New Zealand) on the back of a whale has been lusciously retold for new generations in this exquisitely illustrated book.

Robyn Kahukiwa, a descendant of Paikea, was inspired to write and illustrate the story while visiting Paikea's seaside home with her grandmother. When a few whales entered the harbor, Kahukiwa's grandmother told her it was a sign she must write the book.

Kahukiwa's artwork is derived from her ancestors' art forms, with bold, earth colors, flat symbolic shapes, and black outlines. Most of the patterns in the background, representing the sea and sky, are taken from artifacts from New Zealand's indigenous past. Traditional imagery such as *kowhaiwhai* (painted patterns from an ancient meeting house) and *tukutuku* (designs from woven wall panels) from the east coast of New Zealand's North Island evoke the rich and symbolic history behind this ancient tale.

Born in South Australia, Robin Kahukiwa moved back to her ancestral New Zealand as a teenager. She currently lives in Horo Beach, in a tiny rural settlement called Te Horo, outside of Wellington. Her work is exihibited in both public and private collections throughout New Zealand and overseas. Previous illustrated children's books include similar folkloric tones, such as *Taniwha* (1986) *Watercress Tuna and the Children of Champion Street* (1984), and *The Kuia and the Spider* (1981).

Paikea rode on a whale.

The whale was big and strong.

It saved Paikea's life when Ruatapu tried to kill him,

tried to drown him in the sea. The whale saved him, saved Paikea.

Took him far, far away from Hawaiki,
far, far away from Ruatapu,
the brother who tried to kill him.
Took him to Aotearoa
where he was safe, Paikea.

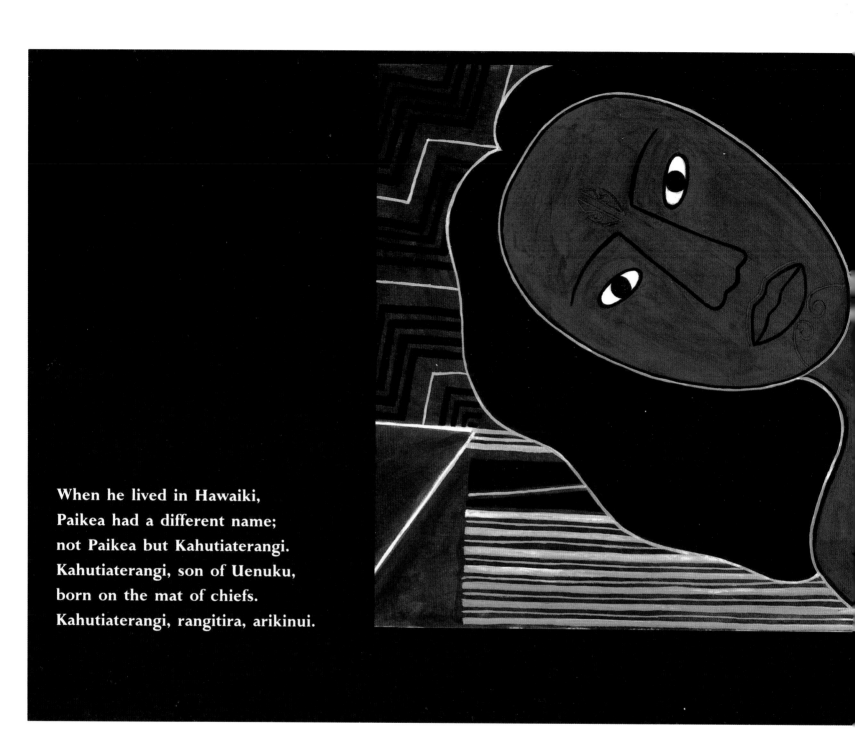

When he lived in Hawaiki,
Paikea had a different name;
not Paikea but Kahutiaterangi.
Kahutiaterangi, son of Uenuku,
born on the mat of chiefs.
Kahutiaterangi, rangitira, arikinui.

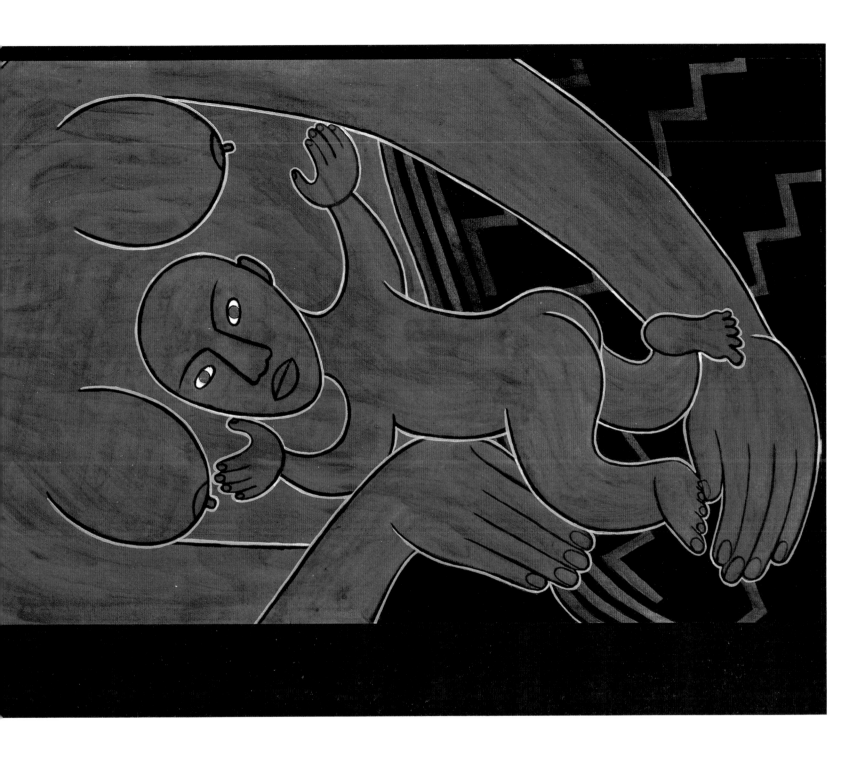

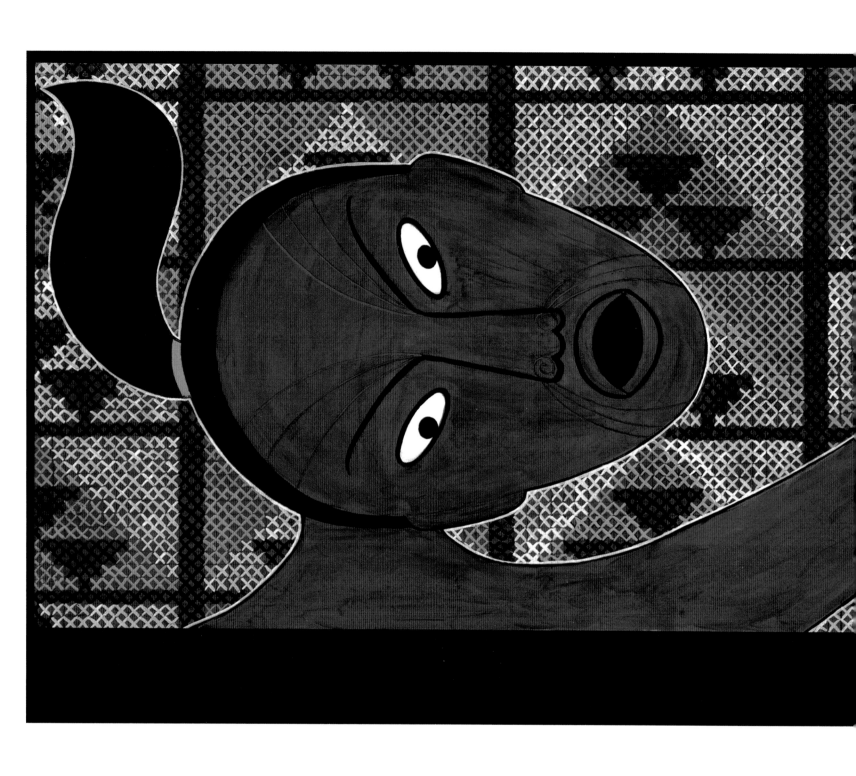

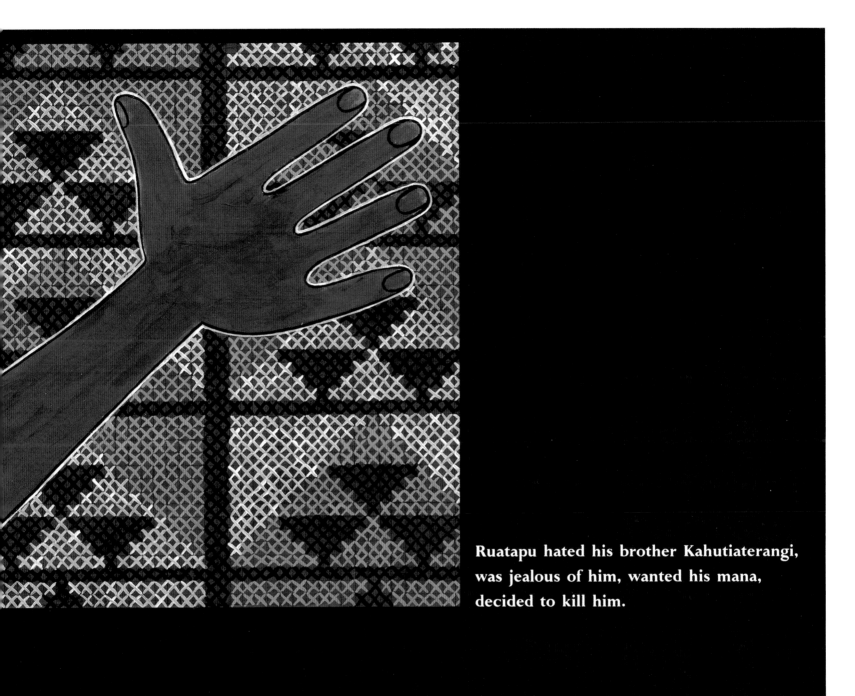

Ruatapu hated his brother Kahutiaterangi, was jealous of him, wanted his mana, decided to kill him.

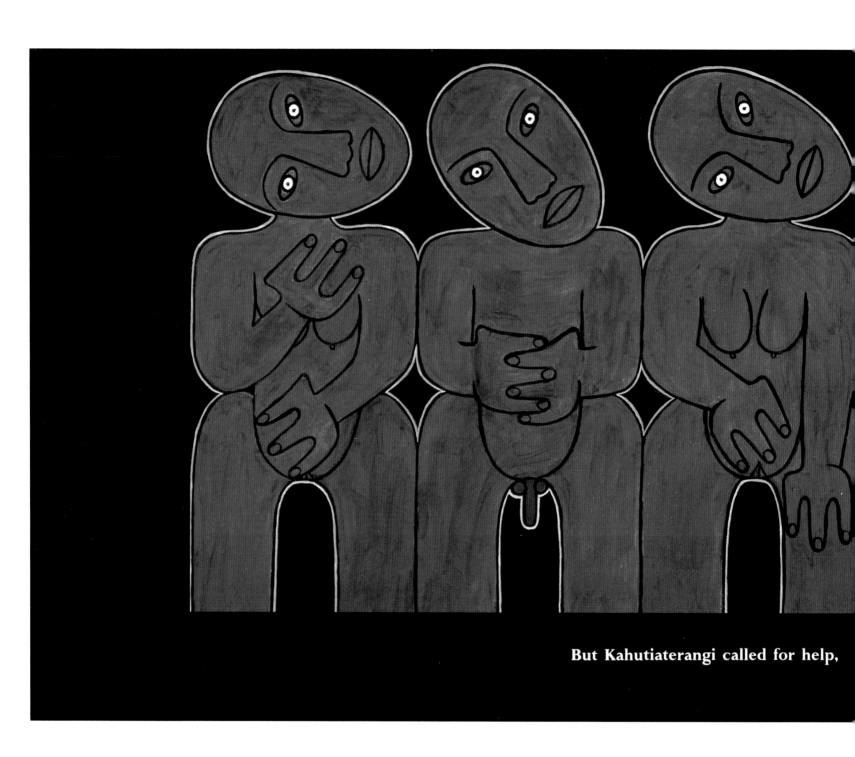

But Kahutiaterangi called for help,

called to his ancestors for help.

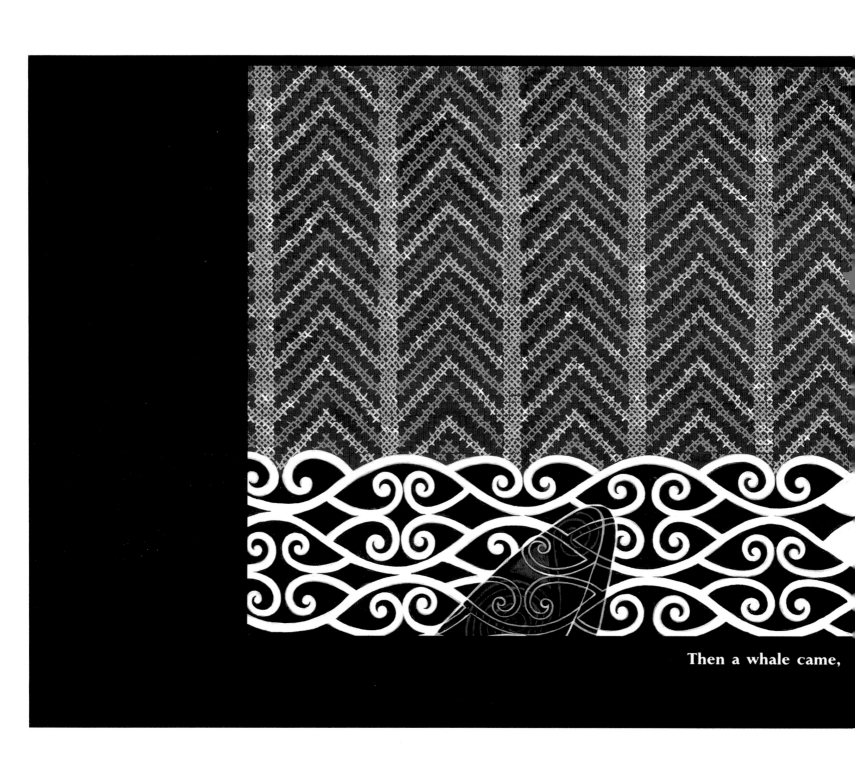

Then a whale came,

a huge whale came.

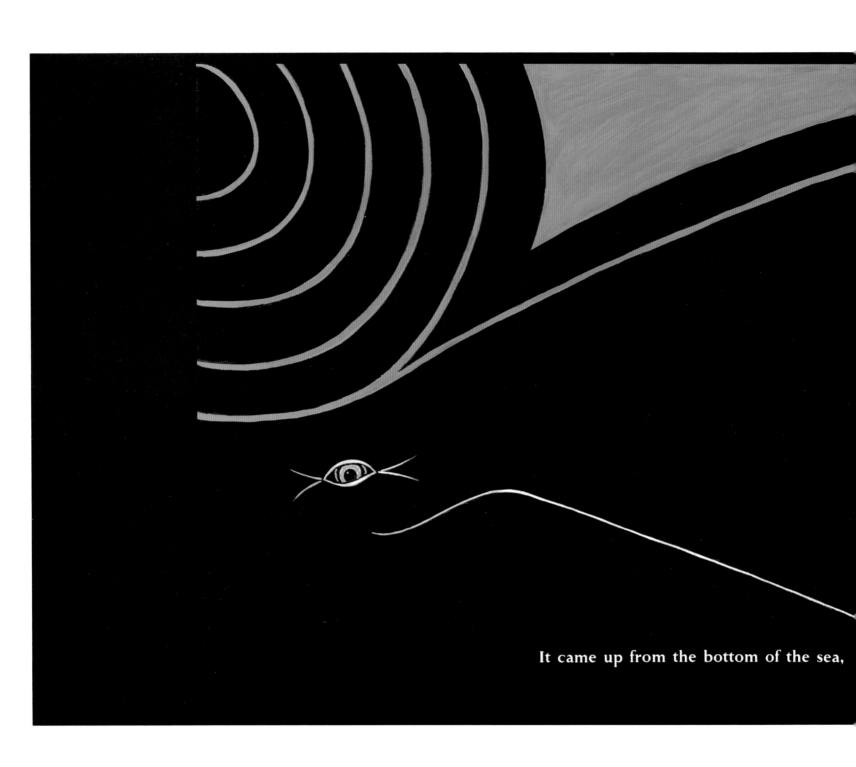

It came up from the bottom of the sea,

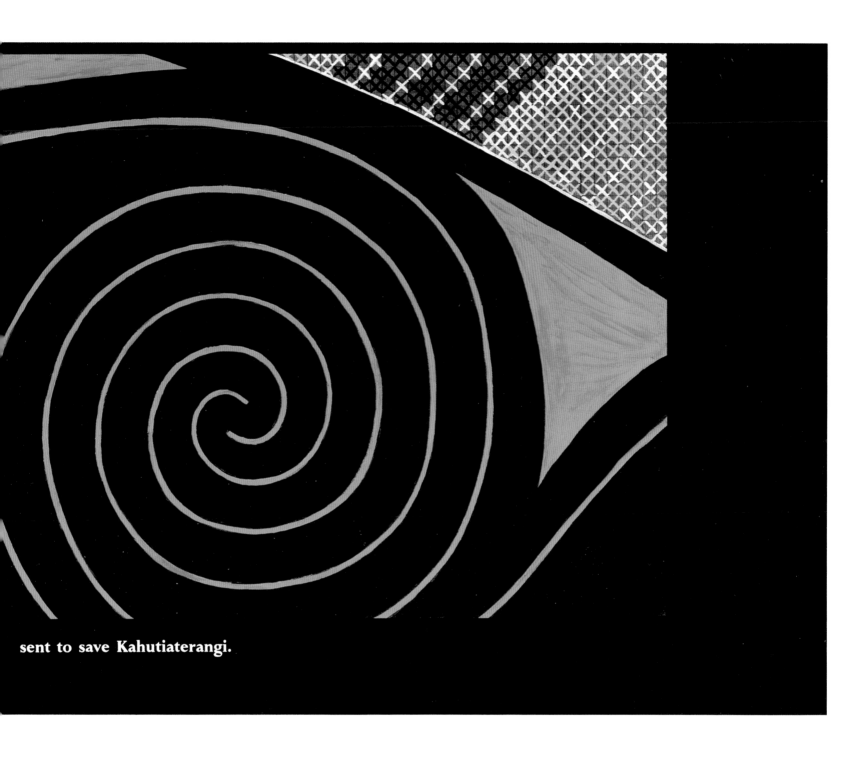

sent to save Kahutiaterangi.

The whale was big and strong,
lifted him up
and swam far, far away.

Kahutiaterangi became Paikea,
the same as the whale.
The whale is Paikea;
Kahutiaterangi is Paikea.

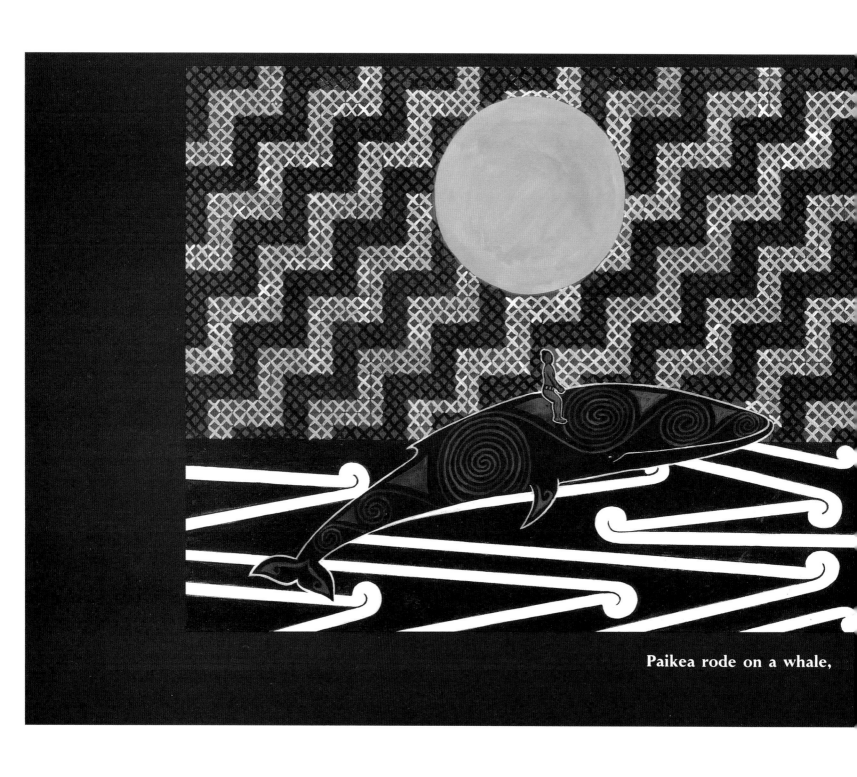

Paikea rode on a whale,

rode through days and nights,

through fierce storms and thunder
    and lightning,
through sunshine and calm seas,
and huge waves and heavy rain.
Paikea rode on a whale.
The whale saved him.

Took him to Aotearoa,
took him to Te Ika a Maui,
kept him safe.

Paikea stayed in Aotearoa,
didn't go back to Hawaiki,
stayed on Te Ika a Maui,
settled at Whāngārā.

He married Parawhenuamea at Ahuahu,
Te Manawatina at Whakatāne,

Huturangi at Waiapu.
He was the father of many children.

Paikea the arikinui,
Paikea the tipua,
Paikea the tahuhu of Te Tairāwhiti.
He tipua! He taniwha! Hi!

The Cat on Pirate's Island (Katten På Sjørøverøya)

Written by Karin Bang

Translated by Mette Line Myhre

Illustrated by Per Dybvig

If you think Puss in Boots was a cool cat, you have never met his brother. Charcoal Charlie is his name, and his tale has never been told . . . until now. Charming and debonair like his brother, Charlie wins the hearts of many with his acts of chivalry, and eventually he wins Blanche, the queen's favorite lady-in-waiting. *The Cat on Pirate's Island* will delight young readers who revel in every detail as they follow Charlie's colorful adventures.

Charcoal Charlie was written by Oslo native Karin Bang, who loves cats and the tale of the famed adventurer Puss in Boots. Bang has written more than twenty books, including adult fiction, poetry, and short stories, which have won various national and commercial awards. This is her second book for children. She lives in an old whaler's cottage on a small island with her husband and, of course, her five cats.

Born in Stavanger, Denmark, in 1964, the prolific Per Dybvig has illustrated more than fifteen books, most of which are children's works. Self-taught, Dybvig is also an illustrator for various newspapers as well as an independent artist with a number of one-man exhibitions to his credit. He counts among his influences various Norwegian illustrators of folktales, and British illustrators, whom he has discovered on his frequent visits to England. He works mainly in watercolor and india ink, which he uses to create brisk, funny illustrations. He currently resides in Denmark with his wife, Monica.

If you like fairy tales, then you have no doubt heard of Puss in Boots. If you know this story, then you probably remember how Puss in Boots tricked the wicked wizard and helped his poor master win the princess and half the kingdom. The cat himself became a statesman.

Hvis du er glad i eventyr, så har du sikkert hørt om Katten med støvlene. Da jeg var liten – det er veldig lenge siden – hette eventyret Den bestøvlede katt, det er sånt gammeldags språk som er nokså rart, men egentlig litt fint også.

Om du kjenner det eventyret, så husker du sikkert at Katten med støvlene lurte en fryktelig trollmann og hjalp den fattige herren sin til å få prinsessen og det halve kongeriket, og selv ble katten minister. I gamle dager måtte man si «Deres Eminense» når man snakket med en minister. Nå var denne katten grå, og ennå er det slik at folk snakker om grå eminenser når de mener folk som har mye makt over saker og ting uten at det syns noe særlig. Og nå vet du altså at Katten med støvlene var den første av alle grå eminenser.

Det hverken du eller noen andre har visst før nå, er at eminensekatten hadde en bror som reiste hjemmefra i ung alder for å søke lykken i den vide, vide verden. Og han var ikke grå, men så kullsvart at alle kalte ham for Feierfrants.

In the old days, one had to address a statesman as Your Eminence. Now, this cat was gray in color, and to this day people still speak of gray eminences when talking about people who secretly exercise great power over things. So now you know that Puss in Boots was the very first gray eminence.

But what neither you nor anyone else has known before now is that this eminent cat had a brother, who left home at a young age to seek his fortune out in the big, wide world. The brother was not gray but black as coal. He was known as Charcoal Charlie.

On the first day of his travels, Charcoal Charlie walked through a deep, dark forest. It was a little spooky, but he just twirled his whiskers, straightened up his tail, and walked right through. He looked so dangerous that neither fox nor wolf dared to come near him.

That evening, he came to a cottage where a poor cobbler lived. He knocked on the door and asked to stay the night.

"Oh, no, I am afraid not," said the cobbler, "for my cottage is full of mice and rats that are eating up both my leather and my thread. I may soon have to move out myself."

Den første dagen gikk han gjennom en diger, mørk skog. Den var nokså nifs, men Feierfrants snurret bare på barten sin, satte halen rett til værs og gikk like på. Og så farlig så han ut, at hverken rev eller ulv våget å komme nær ham. Om kvelden kom han til en hytte der det bodde en fattig skomaker. Der banket han på og ba om å få være der om natten.

– Å nei, det går nok ikke, sa den stakkars skomakeren, – for hytten min er så full av mus og rotter at de eter opp både lær og tråd for meg, så jeg snart må flytte ut selv.

– Det ordner jeg, sa Feierfrants, og på en eneste natt hadde han spist opp eller jaget hver eneste rotte og mus. Skomakeren var så glad at han nesten gråt.

– Nå har du hjulpet meg, hvordan kan jeg hjelpe deg? sa skomakeren.

– Sy et par støvler til meg, sa Feierfrants. Det gjorde skomakeren, og fine støvler ble det, for han var en riktig flink skomaker og kunne vært velstående om ikke musene og rottene hadde ødelagt for ham. Så sa de pent adjø til hverandre, og Feierfrants dro videre.

"I will take care of that," said Charcoal Charlie, and in one single night, he had either eaten up or chased away each and every mouse and rat. The cobbler was so happy he almost cried.

"You have helped me," said the cobbler, "so tell me how I can help you."

"Make me a pair of boots," said Charcoal Charlie.

The cobbler did just that. They were fine boots, for the cobbler was good at his trade and could have been a wealthy man had not the mice and the rats ruined things for him. The two said their farewells, and Charcoal Charlie went on his way.

The next evening, Charcoal Charlie came to a village. There he knocked on the door of a cottage belonging to an old woman. At first, she would not let him in. She had nothing to offer strangers, she said. In fact, she had not had a bite to eat in three days.

"I will take care of that," said Charcoal Charlie. He went down to the river and, in one single night, caught so many fish that both he and the old woman could eat their fill. She was able to salt a whole barrelful of fish for the winter, and still have enough left over to take to town and sell at the market. With the money she made, she could buy coffee and sugar and other good things to eat, along with a pair of new slippers she had wanted.

Neste kveld kom han til en landsby. Der banket han på døren til en gammel kone. Først ville hun ikke ta imot ham, for hun hadde ingenting å by fremmedfolk på, sa hun, og selv hadde hun ikke smakt matsmulen på tre dager.

– Det ordner jeg, sa Feierfrants. Han gikk ned til elven, og på en eneste natt fanget han så mange fisk at både han og den gamle konen kunne spise seg sprekkmette. En hel tønne kunne hun salte for å ha til vinteren, og enda var det så mye fin fisk igjen at hun kunne reise til byen og selge på torget og få penger til både kaffe og sukker og annet godt, og et par nye tøfler attpåtil, for det hadde den gamle konen ønsket seg lenge.

– Nå har du hjulpet meg, hvordan kan jeg hjelpe deg? sa hun.

– Du kan sy en hatt til meg, sa Feierfrants, og konen sydde en veldig fin rød hatt med svart fjær i til ham, for hun var egentlig en flink kone, og det var ikke hennes skyld at hun ikke hadde eid matsmulen i huset. Så slo de følge til byen, og der skiltes de med mange gode ønsker for hverandre.

"You have helped me, so tell me how I can help you," she said.

"You could sew me a new hat," said Charcoal Charlie.

The old woman sewed him a very fine red hat with black feathers. She was a clever seamstress, and it was certainly not through her lack of skill that there was no food in the house. They walked together to town and then said goodbye, wishing each other well.

Charcoal Charlie strutted around town all day, looking very much a gentleman in his boots and his feather hat. He looked at all there was to see, and when evening came, he knocked at the door of a goldsmith and asked to stay the night.

"No, I cannot let anyone spend the night here," said the goldsmith. "Thieves and robbers have been roaming the town the last few days. If they should come here, they might attack the both of us."

"I will take care of that," said Charcoal Charlie. He made himself a bed on the counter of the goldsmith's workshop.

Hele dagen spankulerte Feierfrants rundt i byen som en fin kavaler med støvler og fjærhatt, og så på alt som var å se. Om kvelden banket han på hos en gullsmed og spurte om han fikk være der om natten.

– Nei, jeg tør nok ikke huse noen, sa gullsmeden. – De siste dagene har tyver og røvere vært på ferde i byen. Og hvis de kommer hit, kan de slå i hjel både deg og meg.

– Det ordner jeg, sa Feierfrants. Han laget seg natteleie på disken i gullsmedboden, og da tyvene kom og brøt seg inn, gjøv han løs på dem med glødende øyne og hveste og klorte. Røverne

hylte så høyt at folk kom strømmende til fra alle kanter, og vekterne trengte bare å se etter hvem som hadde klor i ansiktet for å kunne arrestere de to tyvene.

Gullsmeden var så glad at han danset, for nå kunne han endelig sove rolig igjen.

– Nå har du hjulpet meg, hvordan kan jeg hjelpe deg? sa han til Feierfrants.

– Du kan smi en kårde til meg, sa Feierfrants. Det gjorde gullsmeden, og han ga ham både slire og belte på kjøpet. Gullsmeden og Feierfrants skiltes som de beste venner, og Feierfrants dro ned til havnen, for nå ville han gå til sjøs.

When the thieves broke in that night, Charcoal Charlie pounced on them with fiery eyes, hissing, and scratching. The robbers howled so loudly the village people came hurrying from all directions to see what was wrong. The night watchmen needed only to look for scratched faces in order to arrest the thieves. The goldsmith danced for joy, for now he could finally sleep at night without worrying.

"You have helped me. How can I help you?" he asked Charcoal Charlie.

"You could make me a sword," said Charcoal Charlie. The goldsmith did just that. He also made a sheath and a belt to go along with the sword. The goldsmith and Charcoal Charlie parted as the best of friends, and Charcoal Charlie left for the harbor so that he might go out to sea.

Charcoal Charlie was hired at once on a ship called *The Green Parrot.* The captain was in need of sailors and was in a great hurry to set sail.

"I need two men," said the captain.

"I am as good as three," said Charcoal Charlie.

The captain was not a pleasant-looking sort. He was named Long Tom Peg Leg and had a black patch over one eye. His whiskers were so stiff and sharp you could cut yourself on them. To tell the truth, he looked like an honest-to-goodness pirate, which was exactly what he was.

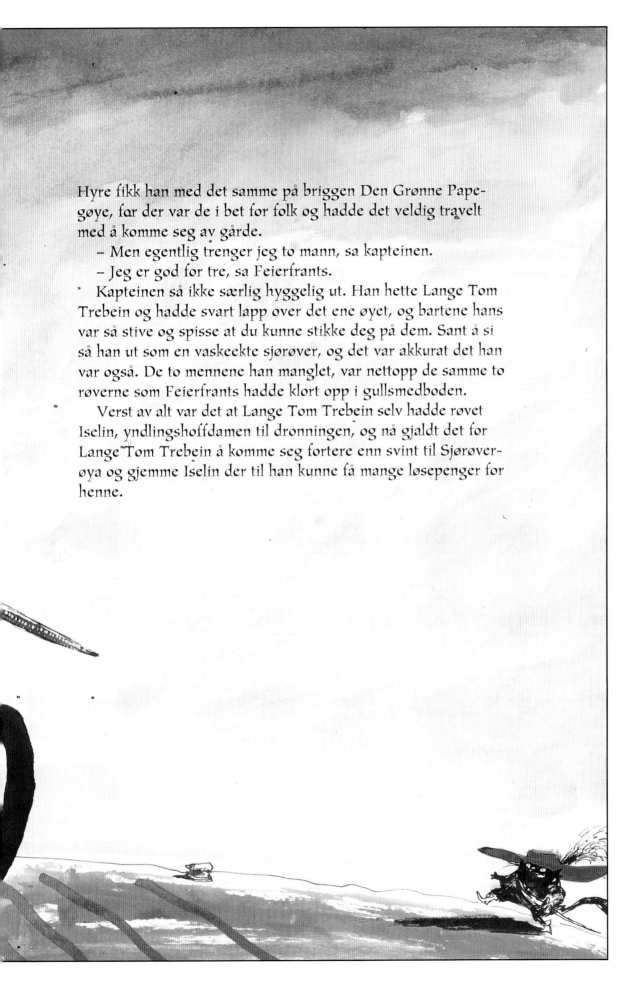

Hyre fikk han med det samme på briggen Den Grønne Papegøye, for der var de i bet for folk og hadde det veldig travelt
med å komme seg av gårde.

– Men egentlig trenger jeg to mann, sa kapteinen.

– Jeg er god for tre, sa Feierfrants.

Kapteinen så ikke særlig hyggelig ut. Han hette Lange Tom
Trebein og hadde svart lapp over det ene øyet, og bartene hans
var så stive og spisse at du kunne stikke deg på dem. Sant å si
så han ut som en vaskeekte sjørøver, og det var akkurat det han
var også. De to mennene han manglet, var nettopp de samme to
røverne som Feierfrants hadde klort opp i gullsmedboden.

Verst av alt var det at Lange Tom Trebein selv hadde røvet
Iselin, yndlingshoffdamen til dronningen, og nå gjaldt det for
Lange Tom Trebein å komme seg fortere enn svint til Sjørøverøya og gjemme Iselin der til han kunne få mange løsepenger for
henne.

The two sailors he was missing were the same two robbers who had been scratched up by Charcoal Charlie in the goldsmith's workshop the night before.

Worst of all, Long Tom Peg Leg had kidnapped Blanche, the queen's favorite lady-in-waiting, which is why he was anxious to rush off to an island called Pirate's Island. There he planned to hide Blanche until he received a large ransom for her.

Poor Blanche sat trapped inside an ugly iron cage in Long Tom Peg Leg's own quarters, looking very unhappy and shivering with fear. Charcoal Charlie found her there when the captain sent him to fetch a compass and sextant.*

"Who are you, and what are you doing in that awful cage?" asked Charcoal Charlie. When Blanche realized that Charlie was not one of the robbers, she hastened to tell him her story and begged him to leave the horrible pirate ship.

"It has to be both of us or neither of us," said Charcoal Charlie. Besides, *The Green Parrot* had already set sail and was far from land. No cat enjoys swimming, even though they can when absolutely necessary.

* Instruments used for navigating at sea

Stakkars Iselin satt i et stygt jernbur i Lange Tom Trebeins egen lugar, og hun var så redd og ulykkelig at hun skalv over hele kroppen. Der fant Feierfrants henne da kapteinen sendte ham akterut for å hente kompass og sekstant.*

– Hvem er du, og hva gjør du i det ekle buret? sa Feierfrants. Da skjønte Iselin straks at han ikke var en av røverne, så hun skyndte seg å fortelle alt sammen og ba ham endelig komme seg vekk fra den fæle sjørøverskuta.

– Begge eller ingen, sa Feierfrants. Dessuten var det for sent å komme seg vekk, for Den Grønne Papegøye var allerede under seil og langt fra land, og ingen katter liker å svømme selv om de godt kan hvis de må.

* Saker som brukes for å finne frem til sjøs.

They had not sailed very far before they were hit by an enormous storm. All the pirates were terribly seasick and unable to do a thing. *The Green Parrot* would almost certainly have been lost in the huge waves if it had not been for Charcoal Charlie. He climbed the rigging and lowered the sails.

Even though Long Tom Peg Leg was not particularly fond of his new shipmate, he had to admit that Charlie had saved the ship, and so he had to ask him what he would like as a reward.

"I want those three barrels of rhubarb wine that are down in the hold," said Charcoal Charlie.

De hadde ikke seilt så veldig langt før det ble et forskrekkelig uvær. Alle sjørøverne ble grusomt sjøsyke og orket ikke å gjøre noen ting, og Den Grønne Papegøye hadde nesten helt sikkert forlist i de svære bølgene hvis ikke Feierfrants hadde gått til værs i riggen og revet seilene, og selv om Lange Tom Trebein ikke likte den nye styrmannen sin noe særlig, måtte han innrømme at han hadde reddet skuta, så han syntes han var nødt til å spørre om hva han ville ha i belønning.

– Jeg vil ha de tre tønnene med rabarbravin som du har i lasten, sa Feierfrants.

Det syntes sjørøverkapteinen var temmelig drøyt, for rabarbravinen som han hadde røvet i den byen de kom fra, hadde han tenkt å selge for mange penger i et annet land (hvor de aldri hadde hørt om rabarbravin). Han skulte stygt på styrmannen sin, men Feierfrants la den ene poten på kården, og med den andre tvinnet han bartene sine så de så like farlige ut som kapteinens, og så måtte Lange Tom Trebein bare gi seg.

The pirate captain thought this was a bit too much. He had stolen the rhubarb wine in the town they had just left, and he had planned to sell it for a large sum of money in another country (one where the people had never heard of rhubarb wine).

Long Tom Peg Leg gave his shipmate a dirty look, but Charcoal Charlie put one paw on his sword, and with the other, he twirled his whiskers until he looked just as dangerous as the captain. Long Tom Peg Leg was forced to give in.

After quite some time, they finally arrived at Pirate's Island. It was a dreadful place—dark and desolate, without a single tree or even the smallest blade of grass. The pirates had hidden all their other booty in a huge cave. They began carrying their newly stolen treasures to the same cave.

Charcoal Charlie was given his three barrels of rhubarb wine, and he at once invited all the pirates to join him in a party. They had not expected this but were very pleased. They thumped him on the back and called him their best friend in the world. Then they all drank and danced and screeched their sinister pirate songs, singing, "Heigh ho and a barrel of rhubarb wine," until they finally tumbled over and fell fast asleep.

Langt om lenge kom de til Sjørøverøya. Den var nifs. Dyster og svart, uten et tre eller det minste lille grønne strå. I en diger hule hadde sjørøverne samlet alle skattene sine, og dit bar de nå alt tyvegodset fra skipet. Feierfrants fikk sine tre tønner med rabarbravin og ba alle sjørøverne på fest. Det hadde de ikke ventet, men de likte det veldig godt. Sjørøverne dunket ham i ryggen og kalte ham verdens beste kamerat, og de drakk og danset og skrålte de uhyggelige sjørøversangene sine om «hei og hå og en tønne rabarbravin», helt til de ramlet over ende og sovnet alle sammen.

Charcoal Charlie got busy! First he cut loose the key to the cage from Long Tom Peg Leg's belt, and then he freed Blanche. Together Blanche and Charcoal Charlie gathered up all the pistols and gunpowder kegs from the pirates and threw them into the sea. With that done, Charcoal Charlie chopped a hole in the bottom of *The Green Parrot* while Blanche loaded provisions on board the dinghy attached to the ship. They rushed to set up the mast and sail and cast off in order to get as far away as possible from the island before the pirates awoke to find their ship had sunk.

Men da fikk Feierfrants det travelt! Aller først skar han løs nøkkelen til buret fra beltet til Lange Tom Trebein, og befridde Iselin. Så hjalp de hverandre med å samle sammen alle pistolene og kruttønnene til sjørøverne og kastet dem til sjøs. Da det var gjort, hugget Feierfrants hull i bunnen på Den Grønne Papegøye mens Iselin lastet proviant* om bord i lettbåten. Så skyndte de seg å få opp mast og seil, og kastet loss for å komme lengst mulig vekk fra øya før sjørøverne våknet og oppdaget at skuta deres var sunket.

Av alle sjørøverskattene tok de bare med seg hvert sitt gull-halsbånd. Feierfrants fant seg et med gnistrende røde steiner som stod til hatten hans, men til Iselin valgte han et med blå steiner, for det passet best til øynene hennes. I tillegg tok de med seg den største og fineste perlen de kunne finne som en personlig gave til dronningen, for Iselin visste at dronningen samlet på perler.

* Proviant er den maten en har med seg på sånne turer som aviser og TV kaller ferder eller ekspedisjoner. Sånn mat som vi har med oss på vanlige søndagsturer, heter rett og slett niste.

Of all the pirates' treasures, the pair took only three pieces. Charcoal Charlie found a gold neck chain with sparkling red jewels to match his hat and then chose one for Blanche with blue gems to match her eyes. And they took the largest and finest pearl they could find as a personal gift for the queen. (Blanche knew that the queen collected pearls.)

They sailed home with a good wind at their backs. When they arrived safely in the harbor, all flags were hoisted, and the cannons boomed a salute. All those who had been out looking for Blanche—no one knew what had become of her—flocked to the ship cheering. The queen herself came running from the palace holding up her skirts to reveal her legs in white silk stockings up to her knees. That was a sight no one had seen before, nor were they likely to see it again.

Poor Blanche had become thin after all her hardship, and her lovely white angora fur had become filthy and bedraggled, but that did not bother the queen. She kissed and hugged her best friend, overjoyed to see her again.

Hjemover gikk det for strykende bør. Da de kom inn på havnen, gikk alle flagg til værs og kanonene skjøt salutt, og alle som var ute og lette etter Iselin – for det var ingen som visste hvor det var blitt av henne – kom strømmende til og ropte hurra, og ut fra slottet kom dronningen selv løpende med et godt tak i skjørtene så bena hennes i hvite silkestrømper syntes helt til knes, og det var noe ingen hadde fått se hverken før eller siden.

Stakkars Iselin var blitt tynn og mager av alle strabasene, og den fine, hvite angorapelsen hennes var både skitten og pjusket, men det brydde ikke dronningen seg det minste om. Hun kysset og klemte bestevenninnen sin så det nesten ble for mye av det gode, for hun var så veldig glad i henne.

– Nå har du hjulpet meg, hvordan kan jeg hjelpe deg? sa hun til Feierfrants som stod der og tvinnet bartene sine.

– Gi meg Iselin til kone og et embede vi kan leve av, sa Feierfrants, og så bukket han så dypt at fjæren i hatten hans feide bakken, og overrakte dronningen den vakre sjørøverperlen som mest av alt lignet en strålende fullmåne, og alle som så den sa ÅH – !

"Now you have helped me. Tell me how I can help you," she said to Charcoal Charlie, who was standing there twirling his whiskers.

"Let Blanche be my wife and give me a position so that I may provide for her," said Charcoal Charlie. He bowed so deeply that the feather in his hat brushed the ground. He then presented the queen with the beautiful pirate pearl, which looked like a radiant full moon. Everyone who looked upon it said, "OH!"

The queen said the same, as she had never before seen such a beautiful pearl. When she had heard about all their adventures, she promised that she herself would hold a wedding for them, but that Blanche must first have time to regain her strength. She decided to appoint Charcoal Charlie to the position of colonel in charge of the royal guards. This was a good position. But first, she asked him to accompany her navy out to Pirate's Island in order to catch the pirates and fetch all their treasures, since he was the only one who knew where they were.

"I will take care of that," said Charcoal Charlie.

Det sa dronningen også, for en så nydelig perle hadde hun aldri sett. Og da hun hadde fått høre om alt de hadde opplevd, lovte hun at hun selv ville holde bryllupet for dem, men Iselin måtte bare få tid til å komme til krefter først. Feierfrants ville hun utnevne til oberst for livgarden sin, det

var et godt embede, men først ville
han kanskje være så snill å løse krigsflåten hennes ut til Sjørøverøya så
de kunne fange sjørøverne og
hente alle skattene deres, siden
han var den eneste som visste
hvor de var.

— Det ordner jeg, sa
Feierfrants.

When the queen's navy arrived at Pirate's Island with Charcoal Charlie, the robbers were actually quite glad to be under arrest. They had had neither food nor water since *The Green Parrot* sank with all their supplies. They all had headaches and could not even stand the thought of rhubarb wine—not that there was any left. They were more than happy to receive porridge and milk, which was much healthier for them anyway.

Da krigsflåten til dronningen stod inn mot Sjørøverøya med Feierfrants som los, var røverne nokså glade for å bli fanget. De hadde hverken hatt mat eller vann siden Den Grønne Papegøye var sunket med alle forsyningene deres, vondt i hodet hadde de, og rabarbravin orket de ikke engang tanken på – dessuten var det nesten ingenting igjen heller. Nå var de mer enn glade for å få grøt og melk, og det var mye sunnere for dem også.

Og da krigsflåten vendte hjem, søkklastet med alle sjørøverskattene og med Feierfrants i merset med dragen kårde – ja, da var alt klart til bryllupet. Skomakeren og den gamle konen og gullsmeden var selvsagt bedt. Skomakeren hadde sydd de yndigste små silkesko til bruden, gullsmeden forærte dem en melkeskål av det pure gull med røde og blå stener i, og den gamle konen hadde laget selve brudebuketten av ville markblomster, og den var så vakker at du kan ikke tro det.

When the royal navy headed home, fully loaded with all the pirate treasures and with Charcoal Charlie at the top of the mast with his sword drawn—well, then everything was ready for the wedding. The cobbler, the old woman, and the goldsmith were all invited, of course. The cobbler had sewn the most charming little pair of silk shoes for the bride, the goldsmith had made a milk saucer made of the purest gold, set with red and blue gems, and the old woman had arranged a bridal bouquet of wildflowers, which was unbelievably beautiful.

The king and queen from the neighboring country were also invited, but the queen had just given birth to a little prince, and they could not make the journey. They sent, therefore, one of their ministers.

And who was this minister? None other than His Gray Eminence, the cat who now saw his brother for the first time in years. He thought that Charcoal Charlie had done quite well for himself out in the big wide world, and found a beautiful wife as well. But Puss in Boots was not jealous, for he preferred his life as a bachelor.

Kongen og dronningen fra naboriket var også invitert, men de hadde nettopp fått en liten prins og kunne ikke komme fra, så de sendte ministeren sin isteden.

Og ministeren, hvem var vel han? Ingen andre enn den grå eminensekatten, som nå traff broren sin igjen for første gang på lenge.

Han syntes nok at Feierfrants hadde kommet seg godt frem i verden, og en nydelig kone hadde han også fått, men han var ikke misunnelig, for selv likte han seg best som ungkar.

Feierfrants og Iselin fikk tre barn. En var svart, en var hvit og en grå. Den svarte ble sjef for kattemusikken, den hvite ble hoff-frøken som sin mor, men da den grå ble stor nok til å stå på egne labber, ble han sendt i lære til ministeronkelen slik at dronningen også kunne få seg en grå eminense. For alle som styrer og steller og regjerer land og rike, er nødt til å ha en sånn en til å hviske seg gode råd i øret – det kommer du nok selv til å oppdage bare du blir litt større.

Og slik ble all ting vel og bra, og alle var lykkelige.

– Det ordnet jeg, sa Feierfrants.

Charcoal Charlie and Blanche had three children. One was black, one was white, and one was gray. The black kitten later became the director of the Purrharmonic Orchestra. The white one became a lady-in-waiting like her mother. And when the gray kitten was old enough to stand on his own four paws, he was sent to his minister uncle to be taught the duties of a gray eminence, so that the queen could have one of her own. All those who govern over country and kingdom need to have someone to whisper good advice in their ear. You will understand this yourself when you are older.

And so everything worked out for the best, and everyone lived happily ever after.

"I took care of that," said Charcoal Charlie.

Григорий ОСТЕР

ВРЕДНЫЕ СОВЕТЫ

«РОСМЭН»

Bad Advice

WRITTEN BY GRIGORY OSTER

TRANSLATED BY NADIA BRUNSTEIN

ILLUSTRATED BY ANDREY MARTYNOV

A well-known author of Russian children's books, Grigory Oster knows children hate to be told to do what is good for them. So he decided to do just the opposite: give bad advice. His cunning and paradoxical rhymes in *Bad Advice* are full of contradictions, but it is understood they are *not* to be taken seriously. We have translated ten of these poems, which prove humor *can* be universal. Kids everywhere will enjoy the wacky and often slapstick rhymes about everything from scaring a houseguest to vandalizing the living-room wall. We hope children will enjoy the poems so much they'll forget to be bad. The witty and often whimsical irony of the verses are reinforced by Andrey Martynov's brilliantly funny and irreverent illustrations.

Grigory Oster was born in 1946 in Moscow. He graduated from a technical college but later studied literature, art, and cinema at the All-Union State Institute for Cinematography and the Literary Institute. Oster dedicated his life to writing for children, but real fame came after perestroika was introduced in the early 1990s. He could at last realize children's book projects that previously had been unthinkable. His three books—*Bad Advice*, *Book of Arithmetics*, and *Book of Physics* (all written between 1987 and 1991)—gained him enormous popularity and were translated widely in Eastern Europe. His other works include screenplays for popular Russian children's films such as *Twelve Cockatoos*.

Andrey Martynov is a young artist, and, although this is his first book, his illustrations are sophisticated and sly. In 1993, both Oster and Martynov received the prestigious Golden Ostap Award for the funniest children's book in the Saint Petersburg competition. They both currently live in Moscow with their families.

Scientists have just
    discovered
that there are
    disobedient children
    in the world
who do the opposite of
    what they are told.
You give them good
    advice,
such as "Wash up in the
    morning,"
and, of course, they do
    not wash up.
You tell them, "Say hello
    to one another,"
and they refuse to say
    hello.
So scientists figured out
    that such children
should be given not good
    advice
but bad advice instead.
They will still do the
    opposite, which means
    they will do
precisely the right thing.
THIS BOOK IS FOR
THOSE CHILDREN
WHO DO NOT LISTEN.

Недавно учёные открыли,
что на свете бывают непослушные дети,
которые всё делают наоборот.
Им дают полезный совет:
"Умывайтесь по утрам"—
они берут и не умываются.
Им говорят:
"Здоровайтесь друг с другом"—
они тут же начинают не здороваться.
Учёные придумали, что таким детям
нужно давать не полезные,
а вредные советы.
Они всё сделают наоборот,
и получится как раз правильно.
ЭТА КНИЖКА
ДЛЯ НЕПОСЛУШНЫХ ДЕТЕЙ.

Потерявшийся ребёнок
Должен помнить, что его
Отведут домой, как только
Назовёт он адрес свой.
Надо действовать умнее,
Говорите: ”Я живу
Возле пальмы с обезьяной
На далёких островах”.
Потерявшийся ребёнок,
Если он не дурачок,
Не упустит верный случай
В разных странах побывать.

When you are lost,
   remember this:
If you tell them where
   you live,
they will just take you
   home.
Do not be dumb. Do not
   ever give your real
   address.
Just tell them that you
   live beside a tall
   palm tree,
with a monkey for a
   neighbor,
on an island in the sea.
If you have a wish to
   roam
and you are not a total
   dunce,
you will get to travel
   more than once
to places very far from
   home.

Nothing is more fun
than picking your nose.
Who knows what might
    be growing there?
If you think it is gross,
do not look—do not
    dare!
I do not pick your nose,
so why should mine be
    your care!

Нет приятнее занятья,
Чем в носу поковырять.
Всем ужасно интересно,
Что там спрятано внутри.
А кому смотреть противно,
Тот пускай и не глядит.
Мы же в нос к нему не лезем,
Пусть и он не пристаёт.

Если вас поймала мама
За любимым делом вашим,
Например, за рисованьем
В коридоре на обоях,
Объясните ей, что это—
Ваш сюрприз к Восьмому марта.
Называется картина:
"Милой мамочки портрет".

If your mother catches
    you doing the things
you like to do best,
    such as doodling on
    the wall,
just explain you are
    only making
a Mother's Day gift for
    her—
a painting you are
    going to call *The Very
Best Mom of All.*

If you want to make
  grown-ups happy,
  here is a method that
  never fails:
At sunrise, start
  screaming and
  squealing and
  whining and nagging
  and kicking and
  running around.
 Be nasty, be sneaky,
  tell lies.
And then, toward
  evening, just stop.
Like magic, the grown-
  ups will smile and
  reach out and
  tenderly hug you, and
  tell you how dear you
  are.

Есть верное средство понравиться взрослым:
С утра начинайте орать и сорить,
Подслу́шивать, хныкать, по дому носиться,
Лягаться и клянчить подарки у всех.
Хамите, хитрите, дразните и врите,
А к вечеру вдруг перестаньте на час,—
И сразу, с улыбкой растроганной глядя,
Все взрослые вас по головке погладят
И скажут, что вы замечательный мальчик
И нету ребёнка приятнее вас.

Если вы окно разбили,
Не спешите признаваться.
Погодите,—не начнётся ль
Вдруг гражданская война.
Артиллерия ударит,
Стёкла вылетят повсюду,
И никто ругать не станет
За разбитое окно.

Should you someday
    break a window,
do not rush to say you
    did it.
Wait a while—a war
    may start,
cannons booming up
    and down,
windows cracking left
    and right:
No one will punish you
for the window you
    have just smashed.

Never, ever wash your
  hands,
or your face or your
  neck, or, for that
  matter, your ears.
It is silly to do it—it is
  useless, for they will
  just get dirty again.
Haircuts too are a
  waste of time:
How long can it be
  before you are bald?

Никогда не мойте руки,
Шею, уши и лицо.
Это глупое занятье
Не приводит ни к чему.
Вновь испачкаются руки,
Шея, уши и лицо,
Так зачем же тратить силы,
Время попусту терять.
Стричься тоже бесполезно,
Никакого смысла нет.
К старости сама собою
Облысеет голова.

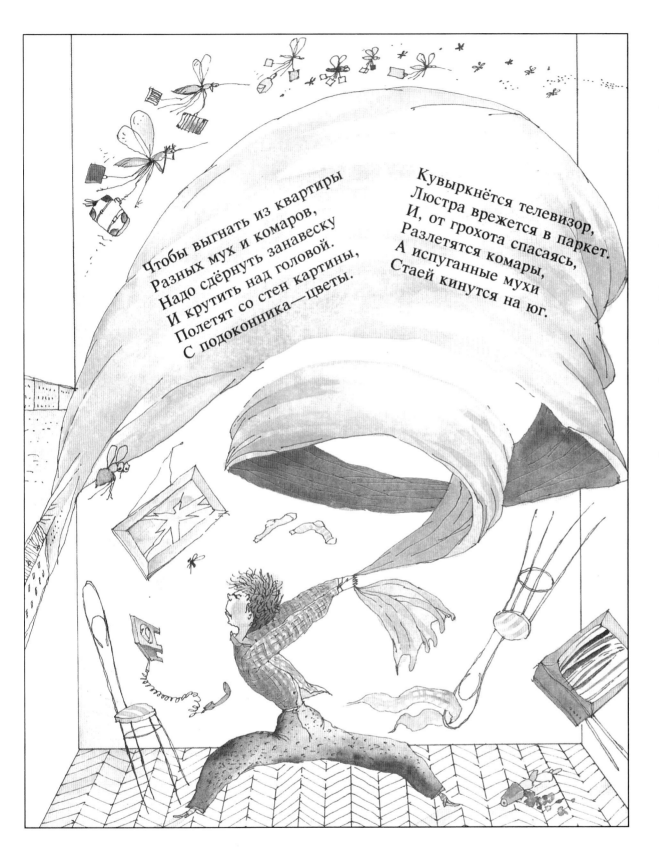

Чтобы выгнать из квартиры
Разных мух и комаров,
Надо сдёрнуть занавеску
И крутить над головой.
Полетят над головой,
С подоконника—цветы.

Кувыркнётся телевизор,
Люстра врежется в паркет.
И, от грохота спасаясь,
Разлетятся комары,
А испуганные мухи
Стаей кинутся на юг.

Want to get rid of flies
  and mosquitoes?
Yank a curtain down
  and wave it around.
Pictures from the wall
  will fall with a crash,
the TV will hit the
  ground.
Every flower vase will
  smash,
and chandeliers will
  shatter.
The mosquitoes, in
  terror, will flee the
  scene
and the flies, in horror,
  will scatter.

Cannibal's Healthy and Tasty Diet

Spoiled Kids with Egg:
Spoil a few kids beyond belief, then coat them with egg yolk, sprinkle with sugar, and, before they start licking each other, serve.

Dried Boys:
Take some boys who will not eat their dinner and hang them in the hallway by their collars. Do not take them down, even if they beg. In a few days, the boys will acquire a most unusual flavor.

Pickled Girls:
Choose some dirty, disheveled crybaby girls, wash them, comb them, and arrange in layers in a sturdy wooden barrel. You may skip the salt—there will be plenty of that in the sea of tears.

Stuck-Up Snot-Nosed Kid:
Drop a stuck-up girl in a frying pan, tell her a couple of times how great she is, and as soon as she turns up her nose, sprinkle with Crisco oil, deep-fry, and keep complimenting while eating.

Если к папе или к маме
Тётя взрослая пришла
И ведёт какой-то важный
И серьёзный разговор,
Нужно сзади незаметно
К ней подкрасться, а потом
Громко крикнуть прямо в ухо:
"Стой! Сдавайся! Руки вверх!"
И когда со стула тётя
С перепугу упадёт

И прольёт себе на платье
Чай, компот или кисель,
То, наверно, очень громко
Будет мама хохотать,
И, гордясь своим ребёнком,
Папа руку вам пожмёт.
За плечо возьмёт вас папа
И куда-то поведёт.
Там, наверно, очень долго
Папа будет вас хвалить.

The next time your
    parents have a guest,
sneak up behind and
scream into the visitor's
    ear,
and say loud and clear,
"Stick 'em up!"
Then watch as she
    tumbles from the
    chair in terror,
spilling coffee all over
    her dress.
I'm sure your mom will
    laugh,
and your dad will be
    proud.
He will probably even
    shake your hand.
And he is sure to give
    you many words of
    praise.

ZAUBERTOPF UND ZAUBERKUGEL

Dušan Kállay

Barbara Bartos-Höppner

The Magic Pot and the Magic Ball (Zaubertopf und Zauberkugel)

WRITTEN BY BARBARA BARTOS-HÖPPNER

TRANSLATED BY LYNN HATTERY-BEYER

ILLUSTRATED BY DUŠAN KÁLLAY

Although this story is reminiscent of a classic Grimm fairytale, *The Magic Pot and the Magic Ball* is a contemporary composition by Barbara Bartos-Höppner. This Eastern European story centers around humans' unending search for happiness: A man and his wife are given a magic pot and, later, a magic ball that bring them good luck. Townspeople learn of their good fortune, and the ball is taken by the mayor for people to use in times of need. When the man and his wife discover that the mayor is using it for his own purposes, they offer the mayor a third ball—one that does *not* bring good fortune. They get their lucky ball back, but not for long, and they must search for good luck and happiness once again. The book's theme is illustrated on the book's jacket: on the front cover people are running toward happiness, and in the end, on the back cover, they are still searching for it.

Dušan Kállay draws upon many artistic schools for his style. His graphic arts background has helped him develop a strong sense of composition. The keen relationship in his work between central motif and detail derives from Renaissance painters. He was also influenced by Hieronymus Bosch and Pieter Brueghel, who both painted folkloristic settings, often with unsettling and strange detail and figures. Brueghel and Bosch are considered the forerunners of twentieth-century surrealism, another artistic school that had a strong impact on Kállay. With a technique that employs gouache, acrylics, and airbrush, Kállay does not make the illustrations mere mechanical renderings of the story; rather, he presents an expression of the text filtered through his intense imagination.

One of the foremost Slovak children's-book illustrators, Dušan Kállay was born in Bratislava in 1948 and attended the Bratislava Academy of Fine Arts. Throughout his career, he has illustrated more than twenty children's books. He is a three-time winner of the Most Beautiful Book of the Year in Czechoslovakia award along with a long list of other national awards for his illustrations. In 1988, he received the Hans Christian Andersen Award. Kállay continues to live in Bratislava and illustrate children's works and exhibits with his solo and international group shows.

Barbara Bartos-Höppner was born in 1923 in Eckersdorf, near Bunzlau, in Silesia, where she also spent her childhood. She began writing as a means of coming to terms with her experiences both during and after World War II. In the late 1960s, she started writing children's stories that speak of tolerance. Her books have received several awards.

BACK COVER

Drüben im Nachbardorf lebte vor Jahr und Tag ein Kirchendiener, der sich mit knapper Not durchs Leben brachte. Deshalb handelte seine Frau nebenher mit Eiern.
Bei gutem und schlechtem Wetter ging sie mit ihrer Kiepe zum Markt, aber Wohlstand war auch damit nicht zu erlangen.
Das eine Jahr schlich sich eine Krankheit in die Hühnerställe. Die Hühner saßen mit aufgerissenen Schnäbeln herum, fraßen nicht, legten keine Eier, kurzum, sie hatten den Pips.
Da sprach die Frau des Kirchendieners:
„So schwer es mir fällt, Mann, ich muß unsere letzte Henne auf den Markt tragen und für das Geld Mehl kaufen, damit ich wieder einmal Brot backen kann."
Also setzte sie diesmal die Henne in ihre Kiepe und ging los. Der leere Magen und der weite Weg machten ihr zu schaffen. Oben auf dem Berg angekommen, mußte sie sich setzen und ausruhen.

Years ago, there lived a sexton over in the next village who made his way through life by the skin of his teeth. Because he and his wife were so poor, his wife had to help out by selling eggs. By both good weather and bad, she carried her basket to market, but even then, prosperity was not within reach.

One year, illness struck the chicken coops. The chickens sat around with open sores on their beaks, not eating or laying any eggs: in short, they had the cheeps. The sexton's wife said, "As much as I hate to do it, husband, I have to take our last hen to market and sell it for flour so that I can bake bread."

So she put the hen in her basket and set off. Her empty stomach and the long journey made the going hard. Upon reaching the top of a mountain, she had to sit down and rest.

Plötzlich sprang aus dem Haselgebüsch ein kleines braunes Männchen hervor. Es fragte die erschrockene Frau nach dem Woher und Wohin, und als sie dem Männchen ihr Leid geklagt hatte, sprach es: „Gib deine Henne mir. Schon lange suche ich nach einem Tier, auf dem ich reiten kann. Ich will dir dafür einen Topf geben."

„Einen Topf?" rief die Frau, „nichts als einen Topf?"

„Warte nur ab", sprach das Männchen, „bis du mit dem Topf daheim bist. Dann wird sich zeigen, ob der Tausch gut war."

Schweren Herzens willigte die Frau ein. Darauf verschwand das Männchen und kam bald mit einem alten, rußigen Topf zurück.

„Dieser Topf wird dir herbeischaffen, was du dir wünschst. Stelle ihn stets an einen dunklen Platz, decke ihn zu und sage:

Töpfchen mein, Töpfchen mein,
was ich will, soll in dir sein.

Nur eines darfst du nicht vergessen, der Topf darf niemals in der Sonne stehen, und du darfst ihn nie und nimmer blank putzen. Vergiß das nicht."

Suddenly a small brown man jumped out from behind a hazel bush. He asked the astonished wife where she was from and where she was going, and after she had told him her troubles, he said, "Give me your hen. I have been looking for an animal to ride on for a long time. I will give you a pot for it."

"A pot!" exclaimed the wife. "Nothing but a pot?"

"Just wait until you get home with the pot," said the man. "Then you will see if you have made a good exchange."

The wife accepted his offer with a heavy heart. The man disappeared and soon returned carrying a sooty, old pot. "This pot will produce whatever you wish for. Put it in a dark place, put the lid on it, and say, 'Pot mine, pot mine, whatever I wish for in you I shall find.' Just do not forget this: you must never place the pot in the sunshine and never scrub it clean. Don't forget."

Luckily when the wife got back home, the husband was busy in the church, and she was free to see whether the little man had told the truth. She took the pot down to the cellar, put the lid on it, and said, "Pot mine, pot mine, fresh milk in you I shall find."

After a while, the wife lifted the lid, and sure enough, the pot was full of fresh milk.

"What luck," the woman exclaimed. "What luck!"

She poured the milk out and began to wish that the pot be filled with bread. After that, she wished for everything necessary for a good meal: soup, a roast, wine, and beer.

The husband's eyes nearly popped out of his head when he came home. "Wife," he cried, "wife, what luck we have had!" And from then on, both of them lived better than ever before—for the first year, for the second year . . .

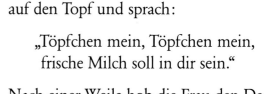

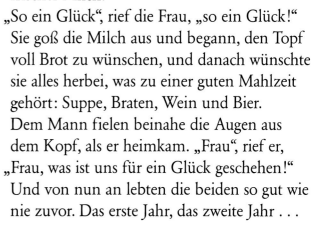

Als die Frau nach Hause kam, hatte der Mann zum Glück in der Kirche zu tun, und so konnte sie sich gleich überzeugen, ob das Männchen die Wahrheit gesagt hatte. Sie ging in den Keller, deckte den Deckel auf den Topf und sprach:

„Töpfchen mein, Töpfchen mein, frische Milch soll in dir sein."

Nach einer Weile hob die Frau den Deckel hoch und wahrhaftig, der Topf war voll frischer Milch.
„So ein Glück", rief die Frau, „so ein Glück!" Sie goß die Milch aus und begann, den Topf voll Brot zu wünschen, und danach wünschte sie alles herbei, was zu einer guten Mahlzeit gehört: Suppe, Braten, Wein und Bier. Dem Mann fielen beinahe die Augen aus dem Kopf, als er heimkam. „Frau", rief er, „Frau, was ist uns für ein Glück geschehen!" Und von nun an lebten die beiden so gut wie nie zuvor. Das erste Jahr, das zweite Jahr . . .

In the third year, however, the wife forgot the rules she was supposed to remember. One day, she scrubbed the sooty pot until it shone and placed it in front of the house in the sun to dry. At that very moment, the pot broke into a thousand pieces. The wife began to cry. She ran to her husband and told him what had happened.

"You must have been possessed by the devil of cleanliness," he scolded. "Now we will have to live in poverty again."

The sexton himself did not want this to happen, however, and when his wife advised him to go try his own luck at market, he found her suggestion better than none. He did not believe that luck would smile upon them a second time. But since it was Easter, he bought a lamb, thinking that it would be easy to sell.

. . . im dritten Jahr aber hatte die Frau vergessen, welches Gebot sie beachten mußte. Eines Tages rieb sie den rußigen Topf blitzblank und stellte ihn vor dem Haus in die Sonne. Im selben Augenblick zersprang der Topf auch schon in tausend Stücke.

Da jammerte die Frau. Sie lief zu ihrem Mann und erzählte ihm, was geschehen war.

„Du mußt vom Putzteufel besessen sein", schimpfte er, „jetzt wird bei uns die Not wieder ein- und ausgehen."

Das wollte jedoch der Kirchendiener selber nicht. Und als die Frau riet, nun solle doch er einmal sein Glück versuchen und auf den Markt gehen, fand er den Vorschlag besser als gar keinen. Er glaubte zwar nicht, daß ihnen das Glück noch einmal begegnen würde. Er kaufte aber doch ein Lamm, denn es war Osterzeit, und deshalb würde sich ein Lamm gut verkaufen lassen.

When the husband got to the top of the mountain, he sat down at exactly the same place his wife had sat—and waited and waited and waited for the little man.

Suddenly, the little man actually did hop out from behind the hazel bush, asked the sexton where he was from and where he was going, and begged him to trade the lamb for a ball. The sexton's heart began beating more quickly, but, coyly, he said, "What, nothing but a ball?"

"You can become very lucky with this ball," answered the little man, and the sexton agreed to the trade. The little man disappeared and came back carrying a shabby black ball.

Als der Mann auf dem Berg ankam, ließ er sich an jener Stelle nieder, auf der auch die Frau gesessen hatte – und wartete und wartete auf das Männchen.

Plötzlich hüpfte es wahrhaftig unter dem Haselbusch hervor, fragte wieder nach dem Woher und Wohin und bat den Kirchendiener, das Lamm für eine Kugel einzutauschen. Dem Mann hüpfte das Herz in der Brust, aber er zierte sich und sprach:

„Was, nichts sonst als eine Kugel?"

„Mit dieser Kugel kannst du dein Glück machen", antwortete das Männchen, und der Kirchendiener war mit dem Tausch einverstanden. Das Männchen verschwand und kam mit einer unansehnlichen schwarzen Kugel zurück.

„Wenn dir diese Kugel einen Dienst erweisen soll", sagte das Männchen, „so lege sie auf ein weißes Leinentuch und sprich:

> Kugel mein, Kugel mein,
> decke mir den Tisch recht fein.

Doch mußt du stets darauf bedacht sein, daß weder Tür noch Fenster dabei offenstehen. Vergiß das nicht!"

Der Kirchendiener nickte nur. Er konnte nicht schnell genug nach Hause kommen.

"When you want this ball to serve you," said the little man, "just place it on a white linen cloth and say, 'Ball mine, ball mine, set this table mighty fine.' But you must always take care that neither door nor window be open. Do not forget!"

The sexton merely nodded. He was in a great hurry to get back home.

The wife had been waiting for him impatiently. While he was telling her what had happened, she put a linen cloth on the table and closed all the doors and windows. Then the husband repeated the magic words. The very next moment, the ball began to spin around, broke in half, and out hopped five, six, seven small men. They set the table with the finest of china and then served a most delicious meal.

After the sexton and his wife had eaten, the small men quickly cleared the table and disappeared back into their ball.

"Who would have thought that we would be this lucky once again," said the wife. "We can live even more comfortably with the magic ball then with the magic pot."

Die Frau hatte ihn schon voller Ungeduld erwartet. Während er nun alles berichtete, deckte sie ein Leinentuch über den Tisch und schloß Türen und Fenster. Dann sprach der Mann den Zauberspruch.

Im nächsten Augenblick fing sich die Kugel an zu drehen, zersprang in zwei Hälften, und aus ihr heraus hüpften fünf, sechs, sieben kleine Männchen. Sie fingen an, den Tisch mit dem feinsten Geschirr zu decken und die köstlichsten Speisen aufzutragen.

Als der Kirchendiener und seine Frau gegessen hatten, hüpften die Männchen sogleich herbei, räumten den Tisch ab und verschwanden wieder in der Kugel.

„Wer hätte gedacht, daß wir noch einmal ein solches Glück haben würden", sprach die Frau. „Mit der Zauberkugel läßt sich noch besser leben als mit dem Zaubertopf."

As could not otherwise be expected, word of the couple's luck spread. The choirmaster heard it, as did the priest and also the mayor. The mayor summoned the sexton to his house. The sexton closed all the doors and windows, told the mayor's wife to get a tablecloth, and then said, "Ball mine, ball mine, set this table mighty fine."

The ohs and ahs were loud, and everyone wanted to own the magic ball. But the clever mayor spoke: "I will keep the ball locked up safe in the money chest and will lend it to anyone who needs it."

"But the ball belongs to me," cried the sexton.

The choirmaster, the priest, and the mayor hurried to promise the sexton everything his heart desired, and finally, with a heavy heart, he agreed.

Wie nicht anders zu erwarten, sprach sich das Glück der Kirchendienerleute herum. Der Kantor erfuhr es, der Pfarrer und der Bürgermeister. Und der Bürgermeister bestellte den Kirchendiener in sein Haus. Der Kirchendiener schloß Türen und Fenster, ließ die Bürgermeisterin ein weißes Leinentuch aufdecken und sprach:

„Kugel mein, Kugel mein,
    decke mir den Tisch recht fein."

Jetzt war das Ah und Oh groß, und jeder wollte die Kugel besitzen. Der schlaue Bürgermeister aber sprach: „Ich werde die Kugel im Geldschrank verwahren und leihe sie jedem von euch aus, der sie braucht."
„Aber die Kugel gehört doch mir", rief der Kirchendiener.
Sofort versprachen ihm der Kantor, der Pfarrer und der Bürgermeister das Blaue vom Himmel herunter, und schweren Herzens willigte der Kirchendiener ein.

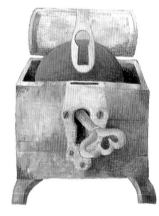

When the husband came home without the magic ball, his wife wailed and shed tears. "It was my fault that we lost the pot. But the magic ball . . . those three gentlemen can now lead a life of leisure and we must once again labor for our food."

So our husband decided to try his luck a third time. This time, he herded two fat oxen up the mountain and did not need to wait long for the little man to appear. "Well," he said, "do you want to have a new ball?"

"Exactly. I let myself be tricked into giving the first one away."

Als der Mann nun ohne Kugel nach Hause kam, schrie die Frau und weinte. „Daß wir den Topf verloren haben, war meine Schuld. Die Kugel aber . . . die drei hohen Herren leben jetzt einen feinen Tag, und wir können sehen, wovon wir satt werden."
Da beschloß der Mann, sein Glück ein drittes Mal zu versuchen. Diesmal trieb er zwei fette Ochsen den Berg hinauf, und er brauchte nicht lange auf das kleine braune Männchen zu warten.
„Na", fragte es, „willst du eine neue Kugel haben?"
„So ist es, denn die erste ist mir auf niederträchtige Weise abgeschwatzt worden."
Das Männchen besah sich die fetten Ochsen und sprach: „Du erwartest gewiß eine große Kugel für die beiden."
Damit verschwand es und rollte kurz darauf eine große schwarze Kugel vor sich her. „Diese Kugel mußt du auf die Erde legen. Der Zauberspruch heißt:

Dreh dich, Schwarze, tummel dich!"

Das kam dem Kirchendiener seltsam vor, aber froh, wie er war, machte er sich auf den Heimweg.

The little man examined the two fat oxen and said, "You probably expect a large ball for the two of them." With this, he disappeared and soon came back rolling a large black ball. "You must place this ball on the ground. The magic words are: 'Spin around, black ball, hurry up!'"

The sexton found these words quite strange, but happy as he was, he set off for home.

Die Frau schloß sogleich alle Fenster, als sie den Mann kommen sah, und kaum war er im Haus, legte er die große Kugel mitten in die Stube und rief:

„Dreh dich, Schwarze, tummel dich!"

Und die große Kugel drehte sich, schnell und immer schneller. Plötzlich teilte sie sich, und zwei Männer stiegen heraus.

Im nächsten Augenblick wurden sie zu Riesen, und jeder schlug mit einem Knüppel auf den Kirchendiener und seine Frau ein. „Dummheit braucht Schläge!" riefen sie dazu.

Das war eine schlimme Überraschung für den Mann und die Frau. Sie versteckten sich hinter dem Ofen, und die Riesen krochen in die Kugel zurück.

Drei Tage später kam dem Kirchendiener zu Ohren, daß der Bürgermeister ein großes Fest feiern wolle.

„Eine bessere Gelegenheit gibt es nicht, ihm den Betrug heimzuzahlen", sprach der Mann und konnte die Nacht vorher schon kein Auge zutun.

When the wife saw the husband coming, she immediately closed all the windows, and as soon as he had entered the house, he placed the large ball in the middle of the floor and yelled, "Spin around, black ball, hurry up!" And the large ball spun around, faster and faster. It suddenly split in half, and two men stepped out. The very next moment, they turned into giants. Each of them began hitting the sexton and his wife with clubs, yelling, "Stupidity demands punishment."

This was a cruel surprise for the husband and wife.

They hid behind the oven, and the giants crawled back into the ball.

Three days later, the sexton heard that the mayor was going to host a big feast.

"There could not be a better opportunity to pay back his deceit," said the husband, who did not get a wink of sleep that night.

The next day, when the mayor's feast was well underway and the small men from the magic ball were already serving the guests regally, the sexton knocked on the door. At first, he was not allowed to enter. But when the mayor heard of the new, larger magic ball, he asked the sexton to come in. "My dear friend," said the mayor to flatter him, "as I can see, you have a new magic ball. It certainly would not cause you any difficulties to surprise us with some new magic."

"Not at all," answered the sexton. He placed the ball on the well-scrubbed floor and said: "Spin around, black ball, hurry up!"

Anderntags, als das Fest beim Bürgermeister in vollem Gange war und die Gäste von den Männchen aus der kleinen Kugel aufs beste bewirtet worden waren, klopfte der Kirchendiener an die Tür. Zuerst sollte er nicht eingelassen werden. Als der Bürgermeister aber von einer neuen, größeren Zauberkugel hörte, durfte der Kirchendiener eintreten.
„Bitte, lieber Freund", schmeichelte der Bürgermeister, „du hast, wie ich sehe, eine neue Kugel in deinem Besitz. Es wird dir doch keine Mühe machen, uns mit einem neuen Zauber zu überraschen."
„Gewiß nicht", antwortete der Kirchendiener. Er legte die Kugel auf den weißgescheuerten Fußboden und rief:

„Dreh dich, Schwarze, tummel dich!"

The guests strained to see as the ball spun around faster and faster. Their curiosity turned into dismay, however, as the ball opened and out stepped two men who turned into giants and began clubbing everyone in sight. While doing so, they yelled, "Deceit demands punishment."

The guests screamed as loud as they could and tried to flee. But the sexton was blocking the door. "No one leaves the room until I get my small magic ball back."

The mayor, who had been beaten black and blue, saw no other solution but to return the good ball. When the sexton took it, the giants stopped their clubbing, became small again, and crawled back into their magic ball. It rolled right up in front of the sexton, and he returned home with both magic balls.

Die Gäste reckten die Hälse, als sich die Kugel schneller und schneller drehte. Aus ihrer Neugier aber wurde Entsetzen, als der Kugel zwei Männer entstiegen, die zu Riesen emporwuchsen und auf die Gesellschaft einschlugen. „Betrug verdient Schläge!" riefen sie dabei.
Die Gäste schrien aus Leibeskräften und wollten fort. Vor der Tür aber stand der Kirchendiener. „Bevor ich meine kleine Kugel nicht wiederhabe, kommt keiner aus dem Haus", rief er.
Da blieb dem blaugeschlagenen Bürgermeister nichts anderes übrig, als die gute Kugel wieder herauszugeben. Der Kirchendiener nahm sie unter den Arm, die Riesen hörten zu dreschen auf, schrumpften wieder zusammen und krochen in die Kugel zurück. Sie rollte dem Kirchendiener vor die Füße, und er ging mit beiden Kugeln davon.

Jetzt begann im Hause des Kirchendieners das sorglose Leben aufs neue, diesmal mit Nachbarn, Freunden und Verwandten.

Eines Tages nun, als der Kirchendiener wieder einmal den Zauberspruch hergesagt hatte und sich die Kugel gerade zu drehen anfing, klopfte jemand an die Tür. Und weil ihm keiner öffnete, machte er die Tür auf.

Im nächsten Augenblick sprang die Kugel vom Leinentuch herunter und rollte zum Haus hinaus. Entsetzt liefen alle hinter ihr her.

Sie sahen, wie sich die Kugel öffnete und die Männchen mit dem kostbaren Geschirr davonliefen, immer den Bergen in der Ferne zu.

Zu der offenen Tür aber sprang jetzt auch die große Kugel hinaus, rollte und rollte. Mit einem Male teilte sie sich, die beiden Männer erschienen, wurden wieder zu Riesen und liefen hinter den kleinen Männchen her, immer auf die Berge zu.

Und bis zum heutigen Tag hat sie niemand mehr gesehen.

The sexton and his wife now resumed their carefree life, this time together with neighbors, friends, and relatives.

One day, just after the sexton had repeated the magic words and the ball had begun to spin around, there was a knock on the door. Since no one answered, the newcomer simply opened the door. The very next moment, the small ball bounced down off the table and rolled out of the house. Everyone followed it, full of dismay. They saw how the ball opened and the small men, carrying their fine china, ran off toward the distant mountains. And then the large ball also bounced out through the open door and rolled and rolled. All at once, it split open, both men appeared, turned into giants again, and followed the small men toward the mountains.

And to this very day, they have never been seen again.

Todos los IRIS al IRIS

MIQUEL OBIOLS

Ilustraciones:

CARME SOLÉ VENDRELL

All the Colors in the Rainbow (Todos los Iris al Iris)

WRITTEN BY MIQUEL OBIOLS

TRANSLATED BY ERIC BREITBARD

ILLUSTRATED BY CARME SOLÉ VENDRELL

Imagine the world without any color—a world of only black and white and, in between, a thousand hues of gray. This situation is the setting for IRIS, a seven-book series written by one of Spain's most beloved writers for children and illustrated by one of the most celebrated European artists today. Each book in the series is set in a different time and place and focuses on a different character. Each, however, takes place "after the Bomb" and includes mischievous little creatures named Irises.

In the seventh book, *All the Colors in the Rainbow,* Rut, her dog, her mother and father, and three scientists explore space aboard the spaceship *IRIS-7.* After a series of strange events, a black border and seven bands of color—"like a rainbow . . . from before the Bomb"—bring back the beauty of color. This unusual tale becomes an intriguing and paradoxical look at human existence.

Because of its careful integration of gray paper, type, and horizontal trim, this series has been praised for its graphic as well as its artistic excellence. (The original design has been revised here due to space restrictions. The original publication featured the text, in white type, on the left-hand page of the spread and its accompanying illustration on the right.) It was named the best children's book published in 1991 by Spain's Ministry of Culture; it also won the Bologna Children's Book Fair's Critici in Erba Prize and made the CCEI honor list in 1992.

Miquel Obiols is a schoolteacher as well as a writer. His books are loved by children, and his television scripts have endeared him to all.

A renowned Catalan artist, Carme Solé Vendrell has more than three hundred books to her credit. Vendrell's work flows from the rich heritage of the Catalan illustrators of the 1930s, which she has adapted in creating her own unique modern style. That style is today imitated by hundreds of younger artists. Vendrell has won numerous awards throughout her prolific career, which spans nearly thirty years, and was a Hans Christian Andersen Medal nominee in 1986 and 1994. She continues to live and work in Barcelona.

After the Bomb went off . . . the sun froze and everything lost its color. And when I was born, the people in space lived in a world of strange shadows.

I was not interested in missions to the Black Sun, and neither was my dog. We did not want to go to the Gray Galaxies either, because it meant having to stay in the space station. We loved to take trips to the imaginary planet or through Saturn's faded rings, hunting for frozen stars and asteroids. Or exploring new passages, like the Milky Way, a kind of highway through space. Seven passengers traveled on board the spaceship *IRIS-7*: my father (R-1, captain), my mother (R-2, doctor), three astronauts (R-3, R-4, R-5, scientists and friends), the dog, and me.

After crossing meandering rivers of milk and picking our way through a silver rain, the ship crashed against a soft white ball.

"We've smashed into a ball of paste!" said some.

"It could be a rubber planet!" said others.

As the spaceship moved slowly forward and struggled to pull free of the doughy mass, I noticed that the planet was made up of millions of tiny creatures. They were so small they were hardly visible, and their eyes were a color I had never seen before.

"It looks like a nest of glowworms!"

"What?" everyone asked at once.

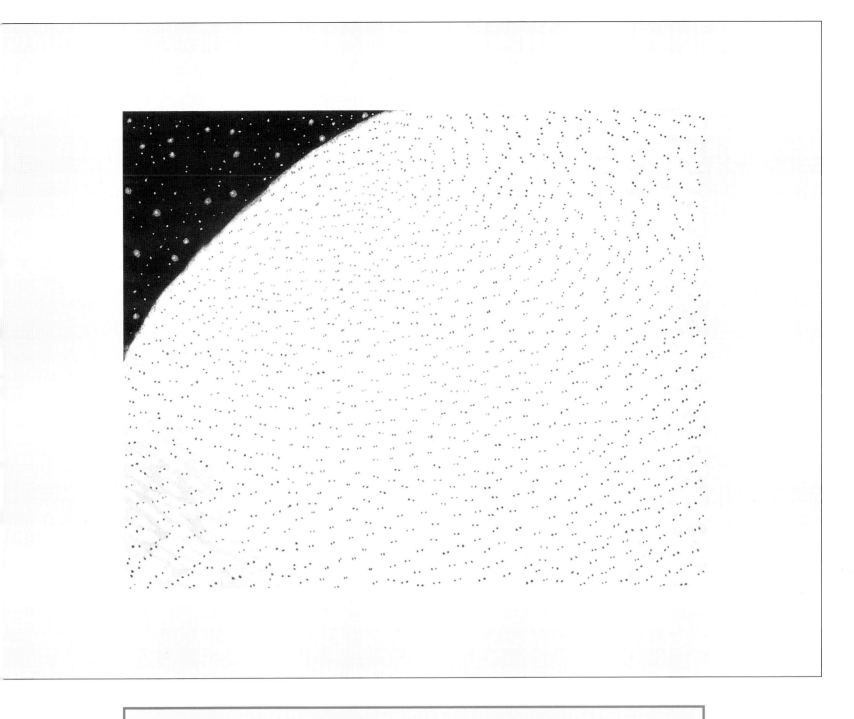

The dog's barking brought me back to my senses. When the spaceship finally came loose, everyone could see that the little bugs were waking up. There were tons of them.

"Maybe it's a space beehive," said some.

"They could be violet spiders!" said others.

The little creatures moved through space with great agility, creating thin strings in a color that had once existed . . . before the Bomb. These purple threads formed enormous spiderwebs.

  We rushed out from the ship in our space suits.

And we started to work: we cut lilac strings, we wound up spools of violet thread. But the more we cut, the more they made. The thread was getting thicker and thicker and the colors more and more intense, until it was impossible to grab one of these amazing cords.

Then we saw the dog, running around in the middle of a huge net of the purple cords. We all clambered down after her, swinging like space people, spinning cartwheels and turning somersaults.

Up in space, time passes in a different way, and it seemed that we bounced
around in that trampoline webbing for an eternity. Until there came a sudden
terrible storm, said some. Or a new bomb, said others.

  The dog leaped into my arms, as if she had sniffed out the scent of fear.
She could tell that something very dangerous was approaching. Since we all
had faith in the dog's nose, we hurried back into the ship.

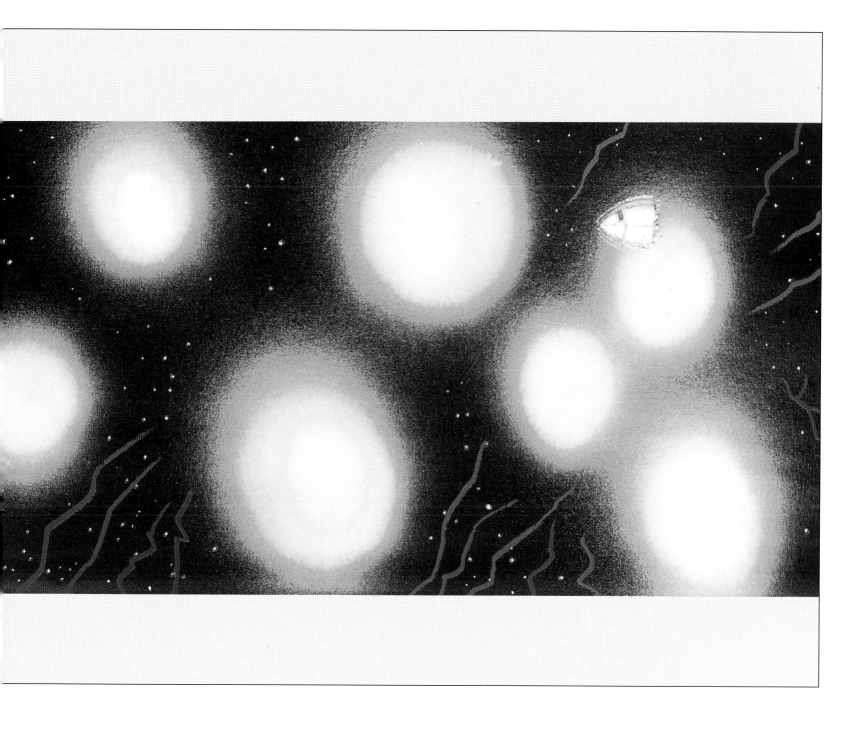

From the *IRIS-7*, we watched the greatest spectacle ever imagined.

First we felt a series of seven thunderclaps. The purple nets shook, and seven giant white holes opened in space. Then another seven hundred and seventy-seven thunderclaps exploded, one after the other, reminding some people of giant firecracker strings . . . from before the Bomb.

Suddenly a tremendous explosion blinded everyone. In that moment, nobody felt sure of their lives, least of all the dog. The spaceship was battered by so many shock waves that I cannot believe I survived to tell you about it. It was a miracle. The seven of us lay in our protected bunks shaking with fear.

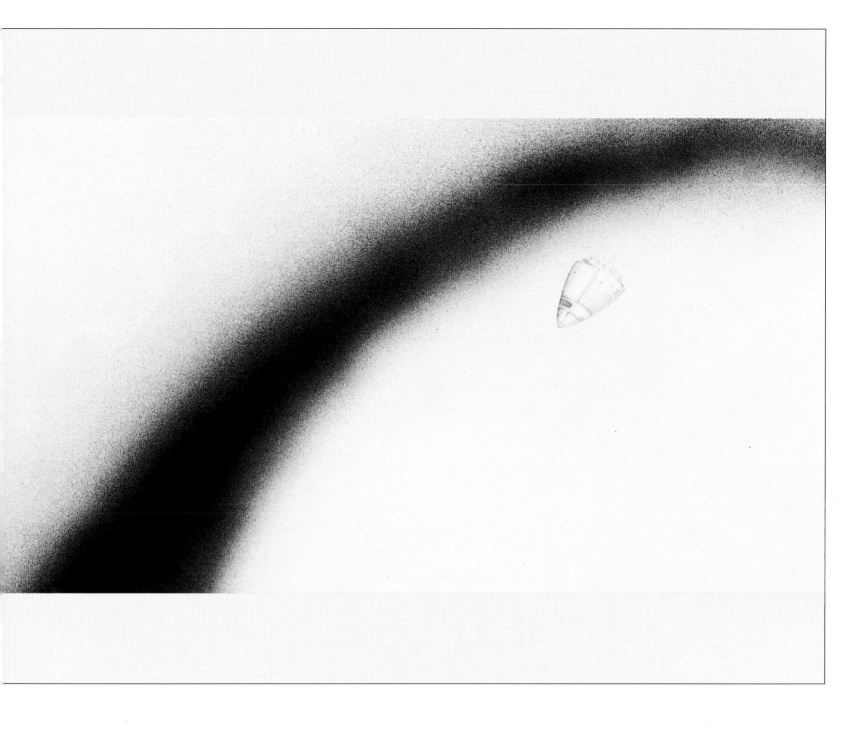

Soon there came a long, calm silence. The white sky opened up, and an infinite black rainbow arched across it, splitting the sky into two parts.

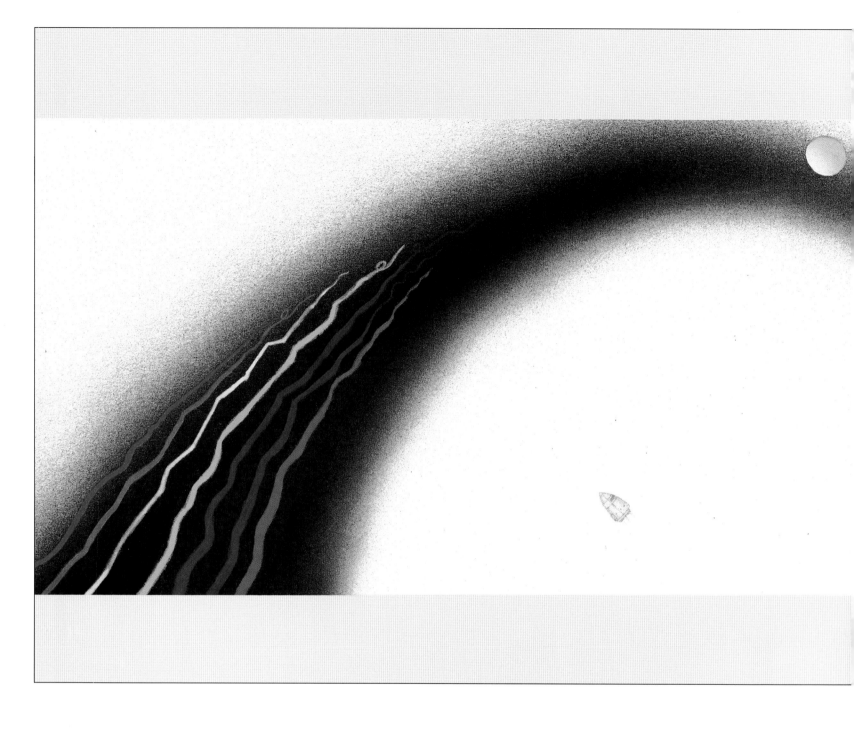

Then followed all the beautiful colors I had never seen. Seven of them, seven colors—RED, ORANGE, YELLOW, GREEN, BLUE, INDIGO, VIOLET. They were disorganized and confused, leaping, dancing, and pushing into the darkness of the black rainbow. It seemed as though the rays of color were fighting to find a good spot for themselves.

Everyone agreed that what we had seen looked like a rainbow . . . from before the Bomb—but I did not know what they were talking about. With the explosion of the new bomb, the rainbow had regained its spectrum. The sun thawed out, and everything filled with color. We were filled with color too.

Except the dog. We were surprised to see that the dog stayed black. But that
was only because she was a black dog.

AN IRRITATED IRIS

IRIS COMES TO LERI

IRIS'S GOLD

EVERY IRIS A DRAGON

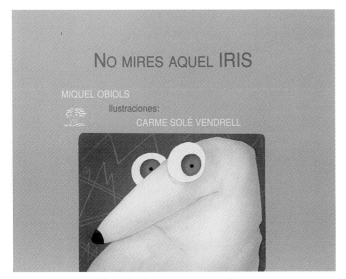

DON'T LOOK AT THAT IRIS

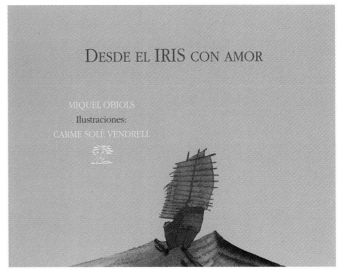

FROM IRIS WITH LOVE

The Umbrella Thief

Sybil Wettasinghe

The Umbrella Thief

WRITTEN AND ILLUSTRATED BY SYBIL WETTASINGHE

Kiri Mama is a naive Sri Lankan villager who goes to town one day and discovers a wonderful invention—the umbrella. Back home, people use banana leaves or sacks to shelter themselves from rain or bright sunshine. Kiri Mama thinks the umbrella is such great contraption he buys one for himself to impress his neighbors. Little does he know that it will disappear—along with every other umbrella he purchases thereafter. Frustrated, Kiri Mama devises a plan to catch the mischievous thief.

The acrylic illustrations are charming in their artistic style, which is characterized by bold flat colors, black outlines, and lack of perspective. The seemingly simple artwork actually reveals vivid details of Sri Lankan life—the colorful clothing of the villagers, the merchandise for sale at the markets, the vegetation of the land—and conveys a sense of the Sri Lankans' close relationship with nature.

Illustrated with black-and-white drawings, *The Umbrella Thief* was originally published in Sri Lanka in 1956—making it the first children's book ever published in that country. In 1986, the book was repackaged in full color and published in Japan.

A self-taught artist, Sri Lankan native Sybil Wattasinghe is a pioneer in children's-book illustration and has more than sixty children's picture books to her credit. Born in 1928, she illustrated her first book at the age of fifteen; it was published five years later. She is the current president of the Indian Section of IBBY and was nominated for the prestigous Hans Christian Andersen Award in 1994. She is also cofounder of the popular children's paper *Bindu.* She credits children as the secret to her success: "Advice from children is a necessity to my work. Before I publish my script I make it a point to read it out to children."

There was once a small village on the island of Sri Lanka.

The people of this village had never seen an umbrella. Whenever it rained they used banana or yam leaves for umbrellas, or covered their heads with . . .

. . . sacks, cloths or baskets. In this village there lived a man called Kiri Mama.

One day Kiri Mama went to town for the first time in his life. Everything was new to him, and he stared about with great curiosity.

"What are those huge flower-shaped things that everyone is carrying?" he wondered.

They were umbrellas which the people were using to protect themselves from the strong sunshine . . . green, red, yellow, blue. Everyone was carrying umbrellas of different colors.

Some were patterned with flowers, some with polka dots and some with stripes. Kiri Mama was fascinated.

"How beautiful," he thought, "and useful too! I should get one to take home."
After a brief search, he found an umbrella shop and entered.
Which one should he buy? There were so many beautiful umbrellas . . .

. . . that he could not decide. He picked this one and then that one until finally he found the one he liked the best and bought it.

He twirled his umbrella delightedly.

As he rode the bus back to his village, he thought with great anticipation about how he would show off his umbrella to the other villagers.

"Everyone will be very surprised. They will all look at my umbrella with wonder and envy."

He smiled to himself with pride, for certainly he was the first person in the village to have his very own umbrella.

By the time the bus reached the village, dusk was falling.

Near the bus stop there was a coffee shop. But there was not a customer in sight as the villagers usually returned home before dark. Only the shop owner and his family were there.

Kiri Mama decided not to show the umbrella to the shop owner. If he was going to show off his beautiful umbrella, it would look best in the light of day.

Making sure no one was watching, he hid the umbrella behind the wall and entered the shop.

Kiri Mama talked about the many remarkable things he had seen in town, but was careful not to mention anything about the umbrella.

After drinking coffee, eating sweets and chatting for awhile, he went outside.

"What? My umbrella's gone!"

A very disheartened Kiri Mama trudged home. The beautiful umbrella that he wanted to show off to everyone was gone. Poor Kiri Mama was so sad . . .

Several days later it rained. And, as always, the people of the village covered their heads with banana or yam leaves, sacks, cloths or baskets.

"If only I had that umbrella," thought Kiri Mama. "I'll just have to go back to town and get another one." And he did.

But once again, while he sat drinking coffee and talking in the coffee shop, the umbrella disappeared.

Still he didn't give up. Each time his umbrella disappeared, he went to town and bought another one. And each time, while he sat drinking coffee on his way home, the umbrella would vanish.

"How strange! What on earth is that thief planning to do with so many umbrellas?" he asked himself. "Next time I'll have to catch the rascal."

Once again Kiri Mama went back to town and bought yet another umbrella. But his time he stuffed small pieces of paper inside its folds.

When he returned to the village, he hid the umbrella behind the coffee shop as he always did.

After chatting for awhile, he went outside and looked behind the wall.

"Are you looking for something?" the shop owner asked.

"No, not really," replied Kiri Mama smiling.

As he expected, the umbrella had disappeared. Saying goodnight to the owner of the coffee shop, Kiri Mama left.

In the moonlight, on the path that led into the forest, Kiri Mama was able to find the little slips of paper which had fallen from the umbrella.

He followed the paper trail until he came to a tree; a large tree which was gnarled and bent like a wise old man. There the trail of paper ended.

Kiri Mama looked up.

What a surprise! From a branch of the tree, hanging neatly in a row, were all the umbrellas he had lost.

Kiri Mama clambered joyfully up the tree.

He dropped the umbrellas to the ground; all but one which he kindly decided to leave for the umbrella thief.

The next day Kiri Mama opened an umbrella shop.

"Umbrellas for sale," he announced. "Get your umbrellas here. Useful in all kinds of weather. They keep you safe from the sun and dry from the rain. Come get your umbrellas here!"

Soon the news spread throughout the village, and everyone rushed to see this new and marvelous thing called an umbrella.

When the villagers walked along the path with their umbrellas opened wide, it appeared the village was blooming with flowers.

"That thief did me a favor by stealing my umbrellas. Thanks to him I could open this store. I almost want to thank him," said Kiri Mama happily as he gazed out upon the magnificent array of flower-like umbrellas.

That night before going home, Kiri Mama went to the forest. He wanted to see what had become of the one umbrella he had left behind.

The last rays of the sun, now falling behind the tall trees, bathed the forest in red and gold light.

Kiri Mama looked up at the branch where the umbrellas had hung, and he began to laugh.

The umbrella was open and sitting inside it was the umbrella thief.
A very unusual thief indeed.

He looked extremely pleased to see Kiri Mama.

And, likewise, Kiri Mama was most happy to see him.

Eveline Hasler   Štěpán Zavřel

Die Blumenstadt

The Flower City (Die Blumenstadt)

WRITTEN BY EVELINE HASLER

ILLUSTRATED BY ŠTĚPÁN ZAVŘEL

Once upon a time there was a small town brimming with flowers—flowers in the parks, in the gardens, in the offices, even in the gas station. One day, the mayor declared that the townspeople would get a great deal more work done if they stopped wasting their time on flowers. Flowers were taken out of the city by the truckload, and any kind of planting was banned. Without trees, shrubs, and flowers, the city slowly turned gray—until the children of the city brought back the flowers and butterflies with their innocent magic. *The Flower City* is a story about the good outwitting the bad, the beautiful overcoming the ugly, flower power beating veto power.

Born in Glarus, Switzerland, Eveline Hasler started writing children's books and adult novels while working as a high-school teacher. She has become widely popular as a writer, especially for her powerful stories about racial and social discrimination. She has won several awards for her books.

Štěpán Zavřel was born in Prague and attended the Prague Film Academy, where he specialized in film animation. He attended the Faculty of Painting at the Fine Arts Academy in Rome in 1959 and later studied at the Kunst Akademie in Munich, where he concentrated on set and costume design for the theater. He then worked for several years in London as art director for Richard Williams, the largest cartoon studio in Europe. A prolific artist, his works have been exhibited in cities around the globe, from Oslo to Mexico City. In 1963, Zavřel illustrated his first children's book, *The Magic Fish*. Since then, he has produced seventeen children's books for various publishers throughout the world.

In 1972, Zavřel cofounded Bohem Press, now a widely respected Zurich publishing house specializing in children's books. Today, in between preparing for gallery exhibits and producing books, he finds time to sponsor educational exhibitions for young artists in schools throughout Europe.

Once upon a time, there was a small town. There was nothing very special about it. The people led modest lives. They were neither poor nor rich, neither hardworking nor lazy. The only remarkable thing about them was that they loved flowers.

Es war einmal eine kleine Stadt. Es gab wenig Besonderes in ihr. Die Menschen lebten bescheiden, waren weder arm noch reich, weder fleißig noch faul. Nur eines fiel auf: Sie liebten Blumen.

They planted flowers in their yards, in buckets, in empty tin cans. They grew them on stairways and balconies and in the courtyards. Even the gas station had flowers. There were also many butterflies in the town.

Sie zogen sie in Beeten, Kübeln und leeren Konservenbüchsen, pflanzten sie auf Balkonen, Treppen und Höfen, ja selbst an den Tankstellen.
In dieser Stadt gab es auch besonders viele Schmetterlinge.

It was always bright there, even on rainy days. The flowers were always radiant. Red and yellow butterflies sailed and dipped in front of the gray walls.

The nights too were never completely dark.

As the people in the little town slept, their colorful dreams sailed and dipped like butterflies through their sleep.

In der kleinen Stadt wurde es auch an Regentagen nie trübe. Die Blumen leuchteten. Gelbe und rote Schmetterlinge gaukelten vor den grauen Mauern.
Auch die Nächte wurden hier nie ganz dunkel. Die Menschen in der kleinen Stadt träumten. Ihre Träume gaukelten wie Schmetterlinge farbig durch ihren Schlaf.

Eines Tages hielt der Bürgermeister der kleinen Stadt eine Rede.
Bürger! sagte er. Ihr verschwendet Zeit mit den Blumen. Deshalb bringen wir es zu nichts. Unsere Häuser müssen schöner, unsere Geschäfte und Fabriken größer werden! Die Kinder sollen mit mehr Ernst lernen! Also weg mit den Blumen! Weg mit den Schmetterlingen! Träume sind unnütz.
Und so beschloß die Regierung der kleinen Stadt, Blumen ab sofort
in Parks
in Gärten
in Büroräumen
auf Fenstersimsen
an Postamtschaltern
an den Tankstellen
und an allen übrigen Stellen zu verbieten.

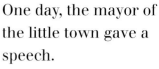

One day, the mayor of the little town gave a speech.

"Citizens!" he said. "You are wasting your time on flowers. That is why we never achieve anything. We must make our houses more beautiful and our shops and factories bigger! Our children should study more seriously! So get rid of these flowers! Get rid of the butterflies! Dreams are useless!"

And so the government of the little town forbade the growing of flowers

> in parks
> in gardens
> in offices
> on windowsills
> behind post-office
> counters
> in gas stations
> and everywhere
> else

immediately.

Now the little town saw more garbage trucks than ever before. One after the other, they drove by, laden with flowers, shrubs, and trees, carrying them out of the town.

Policemen with nets chased after the butterflies.

Far away from the town, flowers, shrubs, and trees were planted in a field, and a wall was built around it. Boxes were hung on the inside of the wall. Butterflies were pinned behind glass in those boxes, labeled with names and numbers.

The people in the town called the field the dream cemetery.

Jetzt gab es in der kleinen Stadt eine noch niegesehene Müllabfuhr. Müllwagen auf Müllwagen fuhr hochbeladen mit Blumen, Sträuchern, Bäumen aus der Stadt hinaus. Ordnungshüter machten mit Netzen Jagd auf Schmetterlinge. Weit draußen vor der Stadt pflanzte man die Blumen, Sträucher und Bäume in ein Feld. Um das Feld herum wurde eine Mauer errichtet. An der Mauer hingen Kästchen. Sie enthielten aufgespießte Schmetterlinge mit Namen und Nummern. Friedhof der Träume, sagten die Leute dem Feld.

Without trees, shrubs, and flowers, the town turned gray. Tall buildings sprang up everywhere. There were traffic jams in the streets. The people hurried past one another, thinking of nothing except work, work, work.

The people did not dream anymore, and without dreams the nights grew pitch-dark. They fell like black sheets onto the sleeping bodies and wrapped them in darkness.

Ohne Bäume, Sträucher und Blumen wurde die kleine Stadt grau. Hochhäuser schossen auf. In den Straßen stauten sich die Autos. Die Menschen eilten aneinander vorbei. Sie dachten nur noch an ihre Arbeit.
Die Menschen träumten nicht mehr. Die Nächte ohne Träume wurden stockdunkel. Sie fielen wie schwarze Tücher auf die Schlafenden herab und hüllten sie ein.

"How boring this town is now," said the children to each other. One rarely heard them laughing. "There aren't any flowers or butterflies," Karin said to Peter on the way to school. "We have to do something before it is too late," said Peter.

That morning, the teacher discovered three flowers on the blackboard. Someone had drawn them with chalk next to the arithmetic lesson.

The teacher was frightened. "Away with this mischief!" he shouted. And with his sleeve he quickly wiped the flowers off the blackboard.

But the next day, new flowers appeared, and more the day after, sprouting among the numbers and words.

In der Stadt ist es langweilig geworden, sagten die Kinder zueinander. Man hörte sie nur noch selten lachen.
Die Blumen und Schmetterlinge fehlen, sagte Karin zu Peter auf dem Schulweg.
Wir müssen etwas unternehmen, bevor es zu spät ist, sagte Peter.
An diesem Morgen entdeckte der Lehrer an der Wandtafel drei Blumen. Jemand hatte sie mit Kreidestrichen neben die Rechnungen gezeichnet.
Der Lehrer erschrak. Fort mit dem Unfug! rief er.
Dann wischte er mit dem Ärmel rasch die Kreideblumen weg. Aber an den nächsten Tagen waren neue Blumen da. Sie sproßten zwischen Rechnungen und Sätzen.

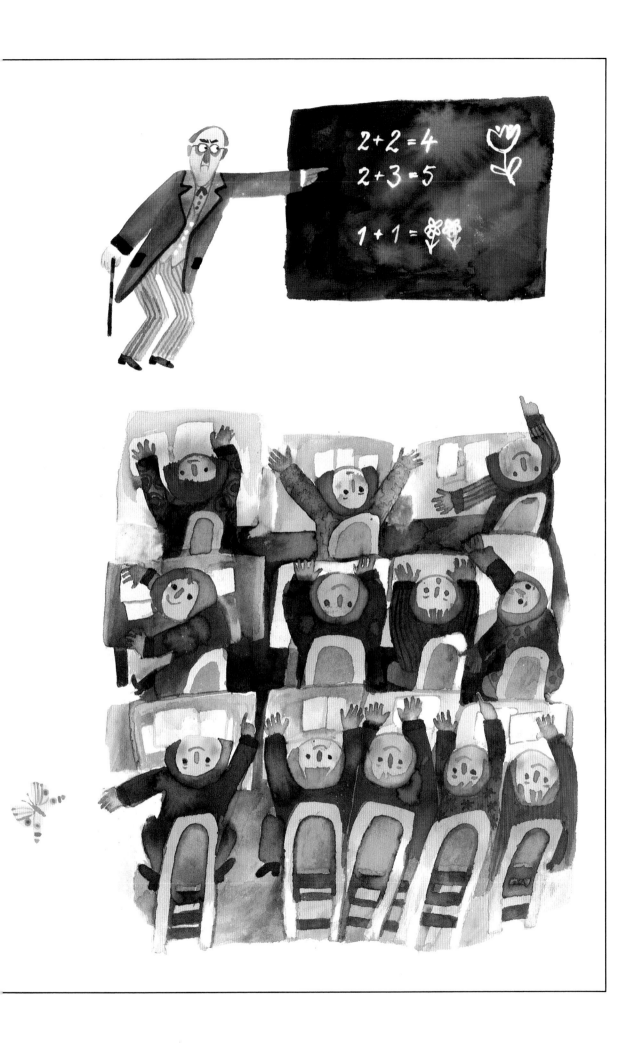

One day, as the children were leaning over their drawing pads, the teacher discoverd a picture of a butterfly.

"Peter, did you do that?"

The teacher leaned over the drawing pad. "What?" asked Peter.

And at that moment, the butterfly was gone.

After the break, during the arithmetic lesson, a butterfly suddenly fluttered over the heads of the children.

"Oh, how beautiful!" cried a girl.

"Catch it!" shouted the teacher.

But the butterfly was already flying through the open window and across the yard.

Einmal, als sich die Kinder über ihre Zeichenblätter beugten, entdeckte der Lehrer auf einem Zeichenblatt einen Schmetterling.
Peter, hast du das gemacht?
Der Lehrer beugte sich über das Blatt. Was? fragte Peter. Da war der Schmetterling weg.
Nach der Pause, in der Rechenstunde, flog plötzlich ein Schmetterling über den Köpfen.
Oh wie schön! rief ein Mädchen.
Fangt ihn! rief der Lehrer.
Da flog der Schmetterling aus dem offenen Fenster über den Schulplatz.
Auch viele Erwachsene wünschten sich die Blumen zurück. Man flüsterte:
Fräulein Rosalie, die Schneiderin, ziehe ein Gänseblümchen in einem Fingerhut. Im Zahnglas in der Fabrikkantine stehe ein Krokus. Herr Dagobert am Schalter sieben im Postamt ziehe eine Blume im Kopf. Sie benötige weder Wasser noch Nährsalz, Herr Dagobert brauche nur an sie zu denken. Und das mache er gerne.

Many grown-ups also wanted the flowers back. They whispered among themselves.

Miss Rosie, the seamstress, was said to be cultivating a daisy in a thimble.

A crocus was said to be growing in a glass in the factory canteen.

Mr. Dagobert behind counter seven in the post office was supposed to have raised a flower in his head, a flower that needed neither water nor earth. Supposedly all it needed was Mr. Dagobert's thoughts, and supposedly he liked to think of his flower.

"We have to clamp down harder," said the mayor. He invited all the police-men to dinner and gave a long speech.

That evening, Karin and Peter secretly left the town and went to the dream cemetery.

Only a few guards were there. The rest were having dinner with the mayor.

"How do we get in?" the children wondered.

The gate was locked, and glass splinters were implanted in the wall.

Then Karin saw a cat slipping through a hole in the wall. The hole was quite narrow, but Karin managed to squeeze through. On the other side, she removed some stones so Peter could slip through as well. Now they were standing in the garden of dreams filled with flowers, shrubs, and trees of the little town.

"How still they are," said Karin. "They look as if they were made of wax."

"But they are still alive," said Peter, point-ing at a blossom.

Wir müssen strenger durchgreifen, sagte der Bürgermeister. Er lud alle Ordnungshüter zu einem Essen ein und hielt eine lange Rede.
An diesem Abend schlichen Karin und Peter zum Friedhof der Träume hinaus.
Nur wenige Wächter waren da, die andern tafelten beim Bürgermeister.
Wie kommen wir hinein? dachten die Kinder. Das Portal war verschlossen.
In der Mauer steckten Glasscherben.
Da sah Karin, wie eine Katze durch ein Loch in der Mauer schlüpfte. Das Loch war ziemlich eng, aber Karin drängte sich durch. Auf der andern Seite machte sie Steine weg und half Peter durchschlüpfen. Jetzt standen sie im Garten der Träume. Da sahen sie die Blumen, Sträucher, Bäume der kleinen Stadt.
Wie still sie dastehen, sagte Karin.
Sie sehen aus wie aus Wachs. Aber sie leben noch, sagte Peter und zeigte auf eine Blüte.

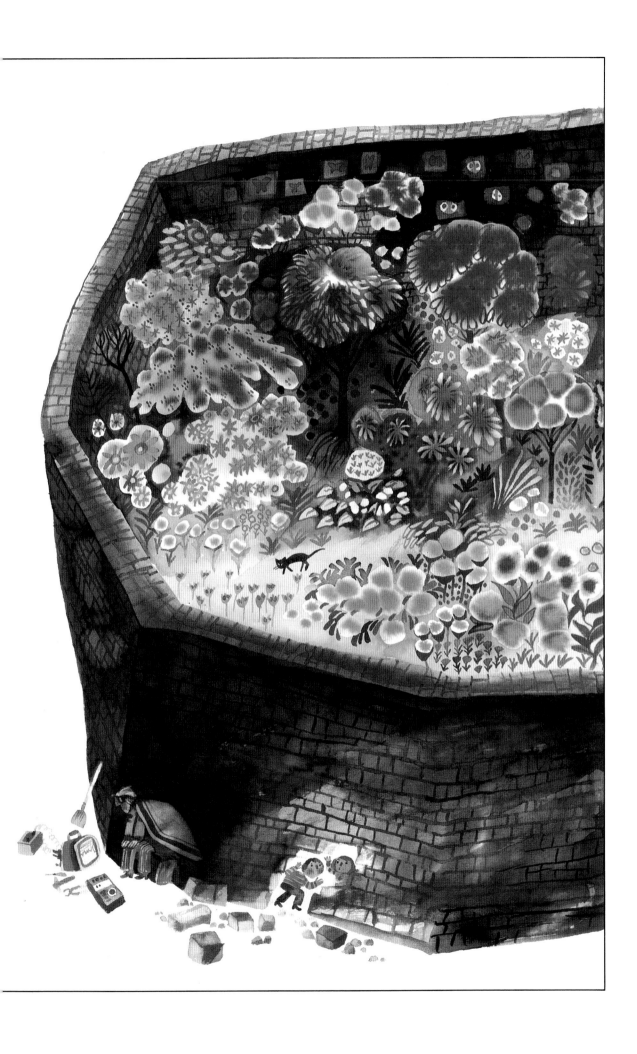

They found the boxes full of butterflies hanging on the wall. Peter picked up a stone and smashed the glass. Karin found the key to the gate hanging on a nail.

The children opened the gate and ran home.

That night, a strong wind blew through the garden of dreams. It moved the trees, shrubs, and flowers. Yellow clouds drifted over the town.

An der Mauer fanden sie die Kästen mit den Schmetterlingen. Peter hob einen Stein auf und zertrümmerte das Glas. Karin entdeckte an einem Nagel den Schlüssel für das Tor. Die Kinder schlossen auf und rannten nach Hause. In dieser Nacht wehte ein Sturmwind über den Garten der Träume. Er bewegte die Bäume, Sträucher und Blumen. Gelbe Wolken trieben über die Stadt hin.

After a few days, plants started to sprout in the little town. A greening and blossoming bustle began

in parks
in gardens
in offices
on windowsills
behind post-office
  counters
in gas stations
and everywhere
  else!

The policemen threw away their hats and fled.

Nach ein paar Tagen begann es in der kleinen Stadt zu sprießen. Es grünte und blühte
in Parks
in Gärten
in Büroräumen
auf Fenstersimsen
an Postamtschaltern
an den Tankstellen
und allen übrigen Stellen!
Die Ordnungshüter warfen ihre Hüte weg und flohen.

The people in the little town were so happy they had a great flower party . . .

Die Menschen in der kleinen Stadt feierten vor Freude ein großes Blumenfest…

which ended in a long
and splendidly colorful
butterfly night.

...und eine lange, bunte Schmetterlingsnacht.

Further Information about the Books

THE BRAGGART LION
Original publisher: Casterman Publishing, Tournai, Belgium
Original publication date: 1991
Original trim size: 5½ x 8"
Illustration medium: watercolor and pencil
Award: UNICEF/Bologna Book Fair Illustrators Award 1992
Sales: As of January 1996, 5,000 copies

STREET SCENE
Original Publisher: RHJ Livros Ltda., Belo Horizonte, Brazil
Original publication date: 1994
Original trim size: 8¼ x 8¼"
Illustration medium: acrylic
Awards: Award Jabuti 1994, from Câmara Brasileira do Livro, São Paulo; Best Picture Book 1994, from the Brazilian Section of IBBY, Rio de Janeiro; Best Picture Book 1994, from APCA (the Association of Critics and Journalists), São Paulo; Biennale of Illustrators, Bratislava, 1995; Octogone d'Ardoise (Centre International d'Etudes en Littérature de Jeunesse, Paris, 1995); and selected for the White Ravens (International Youth Library, Munich, 1995).
Sales: Over 30,000 copies

"JICHANG LEARNS TO SHOOT ARROWS," FROM *ANCIENT CHINESE FABLES*
Original publisher: Tomorrow Publishing House, Shandong Province, China
Original publication date: 1988
Original trim size: 7¼ x 10¼"
Illustration medium: watercolor
Awards: The series won the first award for the Chinese Excellent Children's Readings Prize in 1990; First National Book Prize in 1992; and the Encouraging Prize at the Fourth Children's Book Illustration Exhibition of Noma Concours and the Asian Cultural Center of UNESCO in Tokyo.

Sales: 5,000 copies of the hardcover edition, 10,000 copies of the paperback edition, and 35,000 copies of the popular-binding edition.

THE HIDDEN HOUSE
Original publisher: Walker Books Ltd., London, England
Original publication date: 1990
Original trim size: 9 x 7½"
Illustration medium: watercolor
Award: 1991 WH Smith Illustration Award (also short-listed for the Emil/Kurt Mascheler Award)
Sales: 55,000 copies

DRAGON FEATHERS
Original publisher: Verlag J.F. Schreiber, Esslingen, Germany
Original publication date: 1993
Original trim size: 8⅝ x 12"
Illustration medium: oil
Awards: Luchs 89 (an award given out by *Radio Bremen* and the renowned newspaper *Die Zeit* that honors the integration of design, story, and illustrations of the book) and *Ocotogonales 1994 CIELJ (Centre International d'Etudes en Literatures de Jeunesse*, Paris).
Sales: Published in eleven languages—German, Czech, Portuguese, Spanish, Catalan, French, Swedish, Danish, Dutch, English (both Great Britain and USA)—altogether, the book has sold approximately 55,000 copies.

CAT IN SEARCH OF A FRIEND
Original Publisher: Jungbrunnen, Austria
Original publication date: 1984
Original trim size: 11 x 9"
Illustration medium: watercolor
Awards: Austrian State Prize for Children's Literature and Special Commendation at the Biennale of Illustration in Bratislava, 19851
Sales: Not available

THE LEGEND OF THE PALM TREE AND THE GOAT

Original publisher: Islamic Research Foundation, Iran
Original publication date: 1994
Original trim size: 8½ x 8½"
Illustration medium: ink, gouache, and colored pencils
Awards: Illustrations Honor List award, International Biennale of Illustrations Tehran, Iran, 1994; CBCI (Children's Book Council of Iran) Special Mention, 1995; IBBY Honor List, 1996
Sales: 10,000 copies

FIVE WACKY WITCHES

Original publisher: Ayalot Publishing, Israel
Original publication date: 1993
Original trim size: 9 x 7½"
Illustration medium: watercolor, colored pencils, and ink
Award: The 1994 Ben-Yitzhak Award for Distinguished Children's Book Illustration, one of two national awards given to children's books for their illustrations
Sales: 6,000 copies

PAIKEA

Original Publisher: Penguin (N. Z.) Limited, New Zealand
Original publication date: 1993
Original trim size: 11 x 8½"
Illustration medium: acrylic on fabriano paper
Awards: The New Zealand Library and Information Association's Young People's Non-Fiction Medal and the Russell Clark Award for Illustration in 1994
Sales: About 10,000 copies including both hardcover and paperback editions.

THE CAT ON PIRATE'S ISLAND

Original publisher: Bonnier Carlsen Forlag AS, Norway
Original publication date: 1994
Trim size: 8½ x 11¾"
Medium: watercolor and india ink
Award: Norwegian Ministry of Culture prize in 1994, considered the most prestigious award for children's book illustration in the country
Sales: Approximately 3,000 copies

BAD ADVICE

Original publisher: Rosman Publishing, Russia
Original publication date: 1994
Original trim size: 8½ x 11"
Illustration medium: watercolor and ink
Awards: The Golden Ostap Award for funniest picture book in 1994
Sales: More than 1,000,000 copies sold to date. The three-book series has sold more than 3,000,000 copies.

THE MAGIC POT AND THE MAGIC BALL

Original publisher: Ravensburger Buchverlag, Germany
Original publication date: 1991
Original trim size: 8¼ x 10½"
Illustration medium: mixed mediums of gouache, acrylic, and airbrush
Award: Illustrators of the Year Award UNICEF/ Bologna Book Fair in 1992
Sales: 6,000 copies

ALL THE COLORS IN THE RAINBOW

Original publisher: Aura Comunicación, Spain
Original publication date: 1991
Original trim size: 11 x 8½"
Illustration medium: watercolor, airbrush, and pencil
Awards: Named best children's book by Spain's Ministry of Culture in 1991; Bologna Children's Book Fair's *Critici in Erba* Prize in 1992; and CCEI honor list in 1992.
Sales: 5,500 boxed sets

THE UMBRELLA THIEF

Original publisher: Fukutake Publishing Company, Japan
Original publication date: 1986
Original trim size: 8½ x 11¾"
Illustration medium: acrylic
Award: Most Popular Book award, presented by the Japan Library Association
Sales: Not available

THE FLOWER CITY

Original publisher: Bohem Press, Switzerland
Original publication date: 1987
Original trim size: 8 x 11½"
Illustration medium: watercolor
Award: The Bologna Children's Book Fair's *Critici in Erba* Prize in 1988
Sales: More than 80,000 copies sold in Switzerland, Germany, Austria, France, Faroe Islands, Italy, Slovenia, Sweden, Finland, South Africa (in English and Afrikaans), Spain, and Taiwan.

Editors' Afterword

Enormous amounts of time, patience, and effort went into this project—perhaps as much as creating some of the beautiful illustrations that fill this anthology. We would like to share this rewarding process with you, explaining our selection process and thanking those who have helped my colleagues and me along the way.

For this anthology we received hundreds of entries from all over the world—from South America to Sri Lanka to New Zealand. In order to narrow the selections, we formulated a list of criteria for books to be included: First, the publication had to have achieved critical and commercial success within its originating country; the original publication date had to fall within the past fifteen years; the publication had to be beautifully or creatively illustrated and the illustrations an integral part of the work, rooted in the cultures from which they came.

Unfortunately, much of the selection process was hindered by the mere fact that the book is an international collection: With political unrest, time differences, and language barriers, difficulties in communication and lengthy negotiations, obtaining some of these books were about as easy as arranging a peace treaty.

Differences in paper quality and printing technology also became a deciding factor. For example, many of the submissions from Africa were only in black and white or on paper that could not be reprinted well. Thus a few exceptions were necessary: The entry from Ghana, *A Cat in Search of a Friend* was published not in Ghana, but in Austria. Yet, Ghanan-born Mashack Asare successfully represents the African illustrative tradition that rounds out the collection perfectly.

We hope you agree with us that this anthology is a truly beautiful collection, yet it is by no means a definitive treasury. We have merely scratched the surface, but we believe this sampling highlights the best of the vast and wonderful world of contemporary children's books.

We would like to thank the following people and institutions who helped us usher this project along: IBBY and its national branches all over the world; Julie Cummins at New York Public Library; Dilys Evans; Paula Quint at Children's Book Council; Cary Ryan; Mike Esposito for his extraordinarily diligent hand; Dinah Dunn; Heather Moehn; Vladimir Kartsev at Fort Ross Inc.; Robin Blum at Kane/Miller Book Publishers; Eileen Bogedal at Thomasson-Grant Publishers; Anne Luuka, Mathias Berg, and Waltraud Steeb at Verlag J.F. Schreiber; Christine Castel at Casterman Publishing; Anne B. Bull-Gunderson at Bonnier Carlsen Forlag AS; Geoff Walker at Penguin Books (N.Z.) Limited; Juber Alvares Morais at RHJ Livros Ltda.; D. Ramon Besora and M. Casassas at Aura Comunicación; Antonia Fritz at Carmen Balcells Agency; Judy Burdsall at Walker Books Limited; Susanne Zeller at Bohem Press; Alona Zamir at the Institute for the Translation of Hebrew Literature; Ora Ayal and Ronit Chacham at Ayalot Publishers; Marian Reiner; Noushine Ansari at the Children's Book Council of Iran; Zhao Zhenwan at Tomorrow Publishing House; Frank Jacoby-Nelson, Micha Ramm, and Florence Roux at Ravensburger Buchverlag; Ryan Deussing; and of course all the authors, illustrators, and translators, without whom this anthology would not have been possible.

Publishing Copyright

The Braggart Lion was originally published in French in 1991 by Casterman Publishing under the title *Le Lion Fanfaron.* Copyright © 1991. English Translation Copyright © 1996 Byron Preiss Visual Publications, Inc. Reprinted by permission of Casterman Publishing. *Street Scene* was originally published in Brazil in 1994 by RHJ Livros Ltda. under the title *Cena de Rua.* Copyright © 1994. Reprinted by permission of RHJ Livros Ltda. "Jichang Learns to Shoot Arrows," from *Ancient Chinese Fables,* was originally published in China in 1988 by Tomorrow Publishing House. Copyright © 1988. English Translation Copyright © 1996 Byron Preiss Visual Publications, Inc. Reprinted by permission of Tomorrow Publishing House. *The Hidden House* was originally published in England in 1990 by Walker Books Ltd., London. Text Copyright © 1990 Martin Waddell. Illustrations Copyright © 1990 Angela Barrett. Reprinted by permission of Walker Books Ltd., London. *Dragon Feathers* was originally published in Germany in 1993 by Verlag J.F. Schreiber, Postfach 285, 73703 Esslingen, Germany under the title *Die Drachenfedern.* English Translation Copyright © 1993 by Thomasson-Grant Publishers. Reprinted by permission of Verlag J.F. Schreiber and Thomasson-Grant Publishers. *Cat in Search of a Friend* was originally published in Austria in 1984 under the title *Die Katze Sucht Sich Einen Freund* by Verlag Jungbrunnen. First American edition 1986 by Kane/Miller Book Publishers. Copyright © 1984 Verlag Jungrunnen. American Text Copyright © 1986 Kane/Miller Book Publishers. *The Legend of the Palm Tree and the Goat* was originally published in Iran in 1994 by the Islamic Research Foundation under the title *Afsaneh Derakhteh Khorma Va Bozi.* English Translation Copyright © 1996 Byron Preiss Visual Publications, Inc. Reprinted by permission of the Islamic Research Foundation. *Five Wacky Witches* was originally published in Israel in 1993 by Ayalot Publishing under the title *Hamesh Mechashefot Halchu Letayel.* Copyright © 1993 Ronit Chacham. Illustrations Copyright © 1993 Ora Ayal. English Translation Copyright © 1996 Doron Narkiss and Ronit Chacham. Reprinted by permission of Ayalot Publishing. *Paikea* was originally published in Australia in 1993 by Penguin Books (N.Z.) Limited. Copyright © 1993 Robin Kahukiwa. Reprinted by permission of Penguin Books (N.Z.) Limited. *The Cat on Pirate's Island* was originally published in Norway in 1994 by Bonnier Carlsen Forlag AS under the title *Katten På Sjørøverøya.* Copyright © 1994 Bonnier Carlsen Forlag AS. Reprinted by permission of Bonnier Carlsen Forlag AS. *Bad Advice* was originally published in Russia in 1994 by Rosman Publishing. Copyright © 1994 Rosman Publishing. English Translation Copyright © 1996 Byron Preiss Visual Publications, Inc. Reprinted by permission of Rosman Publishing. *The Magic Pot and the Magic Ball* was originally published in Germany in 1991 by Ravensburger Buchverlag under the title *Zaubertopf und Zauberkugel.* Copyright © 1991 Ravensburger Buchverlag. Reprinted by permission of Ravensburger Buchverlag. *All the Colors of the Rainbow* was originally published in Spain in 1991 by Aura Comunicación under the title *Todos los Iris al Iris.* Text Copyright © 1991 Miquel Obiols. Illustrations Copyright © 1991 Carme Solé Vendrell. English Translation Copyright © 1996 Byron Preiss Visual Publications, Inc. Original concept by Aura Comunicación. Reprinted by permission of Aura Comunicación. *The Umbrella Thief* was originally published in Japan in 1986 by Fukutake Publishing Company under the title *Kasa Doroboh.* First American edition 1987 by Kane/Miller Book Publishers. Copyright © 1986 Sybil Wettasinghe. Reprinted by permission of Kane/Miller Book Publishers. *The Flower City* was originally published in Switzerland in 1987 by Bohem Press under the title *Die Blumenstadt.* English Translation Copyright © 1987 Bohem Press. Reprinted by permission of Bohem Press.